ABIGAIL WALLACE

Alone

First edition

ISBN: 978-1-7352813-0-8

Cover art by Lance Buckley

This book was professionally typeset on Reedsy.
Find out more at reedsy.com

Dedicated to my Grandpa Wallace. Thank you for encouraging me to be creative.
Love and miss you.

1

Chapter 1

After the bombings, I thought I was the only person left in the states. I'm only seventeen, I'm not supposed to be surviving on my own. I mean I guess there could be others out there, although the chances of anyone surviving the attack would be a miracle. But hey, I did right?

If there are others out there they're not anywhere near our campsite in Arizona. I've been walking for almost three weeks with little water and as much food as I could carry in my backpack. I don't really know where I'm headed, but I hope to find somebody out here.

I walk through hot sand, the sun beating down on me. Sweat plasters my dirty blond hair to the back of my neck. My mouth is dry and my head is pounding from dehydration. I know I can't go on like this forever and right now I'm starting to wonder if I should try. I don't see the point in continuing in agony when there doesn't seem to be anything to live for anymore.

I sit down on the dusty ground and unscrew my water bottle. While gulping down almost half of the last water bottle I have, I look up at a large yellow sign with the words "*Welcome to New*

Mexico" written out in skinny black letters. I look at the water bottle. Should I look for more? Should I exhaust myself trying to find more water? The loneliness and sadness overcome me as I sink deep into thought.

I remember that day. I dream about it when I am actually able to get any sleep. It was the fourth of July; the fireworks were coloring the sky, which is why nobody paid any attention when the sound of detonating bombs filled the air. Soon a news report was texted to our phones saying that parts of California, New Mexico, and Nevada had all been bombed. Few, if any people survived the attacks. Every day after that there were reports of other western states being bombed, but nobody had an explanation as to who was responsible for the destruction. Some people fled, hoping to find a safe place to hide, but my family and I stayed.

We thought they wouldn't be thorough enough to bomb a campsite in the middle of nowhere. We were wrong. It was three days after the first bombs went off that Arizona was targeted. Bombs descended upon our campsite. I hid behind my father as he searched for a safe place to hide until it passed. There was screaming and wailing from the others around us. One fell on our camper, I watched it burst into flames. I was paralyzed, my brain was blank. I don't know how I survived. All I can remember was standing in the middle of the chaos in complete shock. I heard my parents screaming at me to take cover...until I never heard them again. I just stood there and watched everything burn, I almost wish I had burned with it.

A couple miles into New Mexico I find a small town, many of the houses have been blown to bits, but I search what's left of the stores for supplies. I find a building to stay in for the

2

night. It looks like the charred walls might be blown over by a gentle breeze, but shelter is shelter. I can't sleep, cold air blows through the cracked windows. I shiver and tuck myself into a ball to keep myself as warm as I can. I wonder if there's anyone else out there. These thoughts keep me from sleeping. I lay half awake for hours until the sun comes up. As night turns to day, I force myself to get up, feeling more tired than before. I know I need more food and water. However, starvation seems so tempting, as morbid as it sounds.

I stumble - my legs weak from exhaustion, but I continue on. I find a half empty bag of water bottles and stuff my backpack full of them. I search through the nearby houses for resources. Of course, when I began my hopeless journey, I would go into these houses and be afraid of finding charred corpses. Now I'm unfazed. They're everywhere, still, lifeless, human bodies. True, it shouldn't seem this casual of a thing, but it's unavoidable. Whoever did all this must be sick, to bomb an entire country, leaving thousands of bodies to rot. Leaving me to see them all.

A sharp pain in my stomach has been making itself more and more known until it becomes unbearable. I stop walking and try to catch my breath. I know it is a mix of the hunger, exhaustion and dehydration. I haven't been meeting my body's basic needs and it's starting to take its toll. I sit down on the hard, rocky ground. I hear faint footsteps coming close, but I assume it is all in my head, a hallucination. I begin to panic. I feel the pain again, like somebody digging a knife into my kidney. My vision fades in and out as a figure approaches. With every blink it draws closer, until eventually I stop fighting it, I relax, allowing my body to go limp. I welcome the darkness that follows.

3

* * *

Slowly I open my eyes, only slightly disappointed that I'm still alive. My head still pounds from the dehydration as I peel my tongue away from the roof of my mouth. I'm lying on an old couch staring at a large pine tree through a hole in the wall.

"Hey there." A boy says; his voice is high pitched, almost childlike. I sit up and look in the direction of the voice. "You didn't look too good when I found you out there." He says handing me a cup of water.

I sniff it to make sure it's safe.

"Don't be so paranoid. I'm not lookin' to kill ya." He smirks. I take a small sip. "What's your name?" he asks.

"You first." I croak, my throat burns as I force the words to climb up and out of my mouth. It's weird hearing my own voice after almost a month of not talking.

"I'm Kevin." I stare at him for a moment, studying him. His long, brown hair is messy and dusty. He has a faded scar, running from the outer corner of his left eye and down his cheek.

Kevin raises an eyebrow, waiting for me to introduce myself.

"Okay, I just saved your life so are you gonna give me a name or I can just make somethin' up?"

"Scarlet." I mumble preoccupied with studying my surroundings.

"What?"

"My name is Scarlet." I say louder.

"Good to meet you Scarlet, why don't you come join me in the dining room and meet the rest when you're feeling a little better." He smiles warmly, leaving through the open door.

"The rest?" I think. *"There are others?"*

Curiosity overwhelms me and I follow Kevin out of the room. I begin to climb down the rotted stairs, afraid that they'll fall out from under me. I find my way to the tiny dining room.

Kevin notices me come in shortly after him. The room of five other people grows silent.

"Everyone, this is Scarlet." He nods in my direction "Scarlet this is Kat, Ally, Evan, Shark, and Alec." he says their names so fast I doubt I'll remember them all.

My attention shifts to the boy Kevin called Shark; his dark hair is messy like everyone else's, but it's a little shorter than Kevin's, his eyes are a solid black. I stare for another moment and then look away. I won't pretend that I don't find him attractive, more than that I find his mysterious vibe intriguing.

I walk further into the room and sit uncomfortably at the table.

The two girls Kat and Ally sit down one on either side of me.

"So Scarlet, where are you from?" Kat asks. She talks fast. I can tell that she is a very energetic young girl. She looks like she's probably fourteen or fifteen years old. She wears her light blond hair in a French braid that shifts just to the right of her head.

"I'm from D.C." I tell them.

"Oh, I've been there! The White House was pretty fancy." she replies eagerly. I just nod and smile.

"I'm from California, but I was in New Mexico visiting family. Ally's from New Mexico." Kat says

"Alec over there is my uncle." Ally tells me. Both girls talk really fast. Like they're stuck on fast forward at all times.

"What about him?" I ask, nodding to Shark who's sitting at the end of the table crossing his arms.

"Oh him? No one knows anything about him. He just showed up a week ago." Kat says.

"Oh." I mumble, looking down.

"He doesn't talk much. We don't even know what his real name is," Kat says. I find myself staring at him again.

"Yeah, we just kinda made something up." Ally giggles.

"So, you all survived the bombings?" I ask, changing the subject. Ally nods.

"Yup, a little bruised up, but we made it." Kat says. "I think all of us have a little hearing loss, though." She giggles lightly.

The girls are charming, but I find myself growing annoyed with them. Maybe it's just because I haven't been around people in a long time. I guess it's good that they can be so positive though, considering the circumstances.

"So." I begin "What do you guys do?" I ask the two girls.

I look around at the house, much of the wood is rotted through. It seems to me like the house has been abandoned since long before the attacks.

The others are sitting in the living room discussing something.

"Nothing really." Kat shrugs. "We spend a lot of time gardening so we have food."

"That's it?" I watch the others talking in the living room.

"Yeah." She smiles. "What else is there to do? Not like we have jobs or anything that needs done."

"I guess not." I frown. There must be something to do though. We can't just be destined to sit here and do nothing until we die.

"Don't worry though." Ally chimes in. "Kat and I are pros at finding fun things to do. We'll help you keep busy."

"Thanks." I reply absent-mindedly. My attention rests on

6

Shark. Currently he is sitting on the floor. His back leaned against the wall, observing Alec and Evan's conversation.

"Like right now." Ally says. I look at her confused. I'd forgotten we were in the middle of a conversation. "You can come help me get dinner ready. That'll keep you from getting bored." She stands up quickly and practically skips off to the kitchen.

I steal one more look at Shark who is now fully aware I've been watching him before following the girls off to help make dinner.

* * *

We all sit in awkward silence around the table eating a small dinner. It's the most food I've had in a long time, so I don't complain. I find Shark staring at me before Ally taps me on the shoulder.

"Yeah?" I whisper.

She smirks and leans over to whisper in my ear, "I think he likes you."

Ally and Kat remind me of my old friends in my Freshman year of highschool. They have a lot of energy and everything seems to be about romance with them.

"No, shut up." I whisper back, still annoyed, but I find myself leaning more towards amusement. Kat looks over and Ally whispers in her ear. Kat covers her mouth and giggles. Shark still looks in our direction, probably annoyed with all the chatter going on.

"What's so funny?" Alec demands, giving the two girls a stern look. They stop laughing immediately and return their focus to the food in front of them.

7

"Is he like, in charge?" I ask, nodding slightly towards Alec.

"Kind of." Kat whispers, she checks to see if he's watching before she continues. "I think this is his house..." She looks to Ally for confirmation.

"Alec took charge right after the bombings, we were having a family barbecue when it happened. His house and his neighborhood were destroyed. He and I just walked until we found a neighborhood that wasn't in ruin. He was in the army before this, was just home for a short while before being deployed again. He's in charge because he knows how to handle this better than the rest of us do." Ally explains. I notice some defensiveness in her voice.

"So... yes then?" I ask.

"Yes, but I'm not sure everyone else sees it that way." Kat says. "I know Evan doesn't."

"What makes you think that?"

"I don't know why Alec lets him stay. He disappears for days at a time and then shows up out of nowhere, usually drunk." she tells me. "Stay away from him, though. He's like all pent up rage and his ego is huge."

"Got it, don't talk to Evan." I repeat under my breath, accidentally locking eyes with him. I quickly look away.

"Then there's Kevin."

"Yup, I've met him."

"He's the best. He's really kind, grounded and super positive. If you're ever down, he's the one you can go to to talk." Kat beams as she talks about him. Alec's turned his attention back to the three of us. I find myself holding my breath as he peers into my soul... or whatever he's peering into.

The dining room falls silent for a second as he scans the people around the table.

"Scarlet, I want you to feel welcome to stay here with us." He says to me, his tone dry. I don't know how to reply. "The girls'll show you where you'll be sleeping later on and if you want, you can join us in working in the garden tonight." I feel like I'm listening to somebody read off the itinerary at a fancy resort.

"Thank you." I finally muster up the courage to answer him.

After the meal I subtly make my way to where Shark is sitting. I sit down next to him and stare at the floor. When I look up I notice him staring at me again.

"Is your name really Shark?" I ask, trying to break the ice. He looks away. "Um... Okay, not a talker then." I mumble awkwardly, folding my hands and resting them in my lap.

I've never been good at starting conversations with strangers, but something in me is telling me to try with this one. I'm intrigued by his silence.

"I'm from D.C." I try again to spark a conversation. Our eyes meet for an awkward moment.

"I know." he replies. I can't decide if I'm happy or not. He spoke for sure, but he didn't say anything. I guess even after everything I'm still a desperate, hopeless romantic.

"Where are you from?" I ask, trying to carry the dead weight of the conversation. He scoots away. I frown. *"Well, I tried, I guess."* I think as I stand up and walk away from him.

"Don't take it personally, he doesn't talk to anyone." Someone says behind me. I turn around to see Evan.

"Yeah, I got that," I sigh.

"I'm Evan, I'm from Nevada, and you're from D.C. Right?"

9

I nod.

I look at Evan to study him as I've studied everyone else. He looks older than me. Nineteen, maybe twenty. His hair is brown and cut short, he's probably about six feet tall. I look at his light brown eyes. Something about him makes me uncomfortable, maybe it's just what Kat said at dinner lingering in the back of my mind.

"So Evan, where were you when it happened? How did you survive?" I ask, trying not to think of what could be running through the boy's mind.

"I don't know, but sometimes I wish I hadn't been one of the survivors," he replies. His words are depressing, his voice is empty.

"Yeah, I know the feeling." I frown.

"I just wish I could get my hands on the person that caused all of this." he growls. I instantly grow even more uncomfortable, realizing I mistook pure hatred for a lack of emotion. Anger pollutes the air around his last statement. I consider responding, but I don't even know how. I freeze, considering my next move.

My next words roll right off my tongue, almost as if somebody else spoke using my mouth, without my consent.

"So do I." I say. "If I could, I would kill every person responsible with no hesitation." If only I could say I was talking like this just to get on Evan's good side, but no, I meant it, every word. A smirk forms on the boy's face after hearing my response. I'm startled by it. Kat said to stay away from him, and I can see why. I sense danger. But, I kind of like it. I relate to him somehow.

"The people here," he begins, "They don't get it. They're just surviving, they don't realize that we need to be doing something, ya know." I can hear the hiss under his tongue.

"We need a purpose." I agree with him. We do need to do something, but what was Evan thinking of doing? "What do you suggest we do?"

"Well, I think we need to track down whoever is responsible and return the favor." he tells me. As nice as it sounds, I struggle to contain my laughter. It's not funny, just impossible. We have no computers, no internet or phones, there is no way to know who did this to us. I just nod.

"We can't just sit around doing nothing."

"No, we can't." I agree. "But I don't think it's possible to find them."

His smirk turns to a kind of frown I've never seen on anyone, his eyes harden. I find myself taking a small step back.

"We could if we tried." he argues.

"We can't do that... but *we can do something."* I find myself thinking. I feel an adrenaline rush like the ones I would get back in school when I was given the opportunity to plan something.

"They don't understand this anger like you and I do, but we can make them understand." Evan's voice is low. I stand in front of him, locking eyes. "You can make them understand." I find myself growing anxious. I've been here for around two hours and I've already made friends with a maniac, and I'm staying in a house full of strangers that I don't even know if I can trust. Not that there seems to be a better option. "

I think they get it." I vomit up, wishing I had chosen better words. "They're probably angry too."

"They won't get it until we make them get it." he insists. "But you do, I can see it in your eyes that you're like me, you understand." There's that hiss again. We maintain eye contact until he finally breaks it and walks away. I let out the breath I was holding in and look around the now empty house. Everyone else is in the garden now.

I stand and think about what Evan just said for a few minutes. Why does he think I can make them understand? What is it exactly that they need to understand? I find myself storming towards the garden. I don't know what I plan to do once I'm out there, what I plan to say.

I walk through the back door onto the patio outside of the garden, Evan somehow managed to get deep into the garden before I followed him outside. I drop the door by accident, making a loud noise that makes everyone turn their attention to me. I walk into the garden to join them.

"Did you really have to slam the only door that's still intact?" Kevin jokes. I roll my eyes at him. "Okay, then." He frowns, taking a step back.

"Scarlet, are you okay?" Ally asks. I feel anger settle in my gut. "You look upset." "

I don't trust you guys." I say bluntly. "I don't trust any of this. How'd you all end up here?"

"Uncle Alec got us here." Ally replies. "Scarlet we saved you, you can trust us."

"Yeah! I saved you from dying of hunger, sleep deprivation and dehydration." Kevin points out.

"Fair," I nod "So you saved my life, but why?"

"Because normal people don't let other people die." Kat answers somewhat sarcastically. "What do we look like? Murderers?"

I shrug. I mean they could be. Alec stares at me in complete silence. I turn my attention to him.

"And you're in charge?" I ask, sounding like one of those

picky ladies in a restaurant asking for a manager.

He shrugs, "I mean, survival is more of a team effort." he replies. "Nobody's 'in charge' we all just help to keep each other alive."

"So, we're just gonna stay here and survive?" I ask, raising my voice slightly.

"What do you suggest we do?" Alec replies sarcastically.

I look at Evan, *"Well, not commit mass murder, but we need to do something."* Is what i want to say to Evan, instead I say something much worse. "You're angry, right?"

He slightly nods his head.

"Let's do something about it. Let's, I don't know, figure out who's responsible for this and blow them up." My eyes meet with Alec's. Evan smirks a bit. The others just stare at me like I'm insane. I probably look insane.

"That's ridiculous." Alec chuckles. "We don't know who's responsible, and even if we did, we aren't all psychotic." He gestures to the others who are scattered around the garden. I pause, staring at the group of people before me.

"I'm not crazy! I just don't like the idea of doing nothing."

"You know, if you don't like the way I'm running things, you can leave." Alec points in a random direction.

"Okay, why don't you just calm down." Shark says from behind me. "We can talk about coming up with a project or something if that's what you need. But you aren't helping your case by starting drama."

I don't even turn to look at him, but I begin to feel myself calm down. Butterflies flutter around my stomach. *"Don't go falling in love Scarlet. You just met him."* I scold myself.

"You literally just got here today. You don't get to start demanding that we blow people up." Alec says, I can tell he's

13

annoyed. "We do have projects though, and if you don't mind, I'd like to get back to one of them." He adjusts his grip on the shovel he's using.

"Well, what about fixing those rotting stairs or floors or trying to find more survivors or something?" I argue.

"You do not get to storm out here, whine about not trusting us, and then tell me how to run things." he growls. I know I may be overstepping, but I need something to focus on or I'm going to lose my mind.

"Let's just sit down and talk about it later." Shark suggests. Alec scowls at the idea.

"That's all I want." I say. I'm much calmer now. I'm beginning to realize that the way I approached this was a bit dramatic, but I just need to be heard on this. "I'm sorry, I don't want to take over. I just need something to focus on. I need a reason to, well you know." I look to the ground.

"Fine, we'll talk." Alec rolls his eyes. "Meet in the living room in twenty minutes."

I smirk, knowing that I won the argument, with the help of mystery boy.

I turn to Shark, I look him up and down. Studying his muscular figure, his dark hair, his deep eyes. I take a deep breath and smile at him. He scowls in return, but I don't mind. He backs away from the door to let me in and then goes back out to join the others.

2

Chapter 2

Everyone gathers in the living room. Alec glares at me as everyone finds a seat.

Kat sits next to me, "Feel better?" she whispers. I ignore her.

"So?" Alec raises his eyebrows in annoyance, "You wanted to talk... start talking."

"This was technically Shark's idea." I retort, but I talk anyway, "Look, we all just went through the most tragic thing we've probably ever been through and you guys are just kind of here, surviving. And that's great. I just feel like we could be doing more. Something purposeful."

"I understand. Trust me, I'm angry too. Going complete psycho and killing anyone that may somehow be alive, however, is a horrible way to go about this." Alec says. I look at Evan hoping to get some help.

"These people deserve it." Evan chimes in. I almost feel guilty for appreciating the backup. Shark sits quietly, observing our conversation, his attention trained specifically on Evan.

"Even if I was as bloodthirsty as you two, which I'm not, we have no way to do that. 'These people' probably aren't even in the country. But how about this, how about you explain exactly how you would go about releasing your pent up anger on these guys? I could use some good entertainment" Alec and I lock eyes, the room grows silent.

I think frantically for an answer, I refuse to look like a moron in front of this guy.

"Why not just blow them up?" I finally say. Repeating what I said back in the garden.

Alec crosses his arms, "You probably don't know a thing about bombs."

I got nothing. He's right, I don't know anything about bombs.

"I do, though." Evan says. Why am I not surprised? "We build a bomb, track them down and boom, karma." He grins. I feel my anger dying down a little. I feel less homicidal, realizing how crazy I must sound.

"Look, I don't care about blowing some people up, but what are you guys doing to stay busy? To make things better." I change my angle.

"For your information we've been gardening and searching for survivors. How do you think we found you?" Alec argues, he turns to Kevin. "You think we can put her back?" he mumbles.

"Okay, I'll admit I didn't know that. But like this house isn't in the best shape and... and, I don't know." *"And I'm bored and need something to do."* I finish in my head.

"You didn't know that because you just got here." Alec balls his hands into fist, his jaw clenched tight. "You know what though? Since you obviously think you know how to do this better than the rest of us, and I'm tired of listening to you talk. Why don't you just take over from here. You are in charge." Alec says."Congratulations Boss." He claps his hands mockingly.

I raise an eyebrow, "Seriously?" I say shocked.

He glares at me. Nobody else in the room moves a muscle, they barely even breathe.

"I do have some ideas." I say, my tone threatening. Alec takes a deep breath, I can almost see the image running through his head of him punching my face in.

"Well, let me just leave you to your 'ideas' then," he growls. He stands up and looks around the room. "You guys have fun with this one." He stomps out.

Tension lingers in the air. I'm shaking, possibly from fear, more likely from excitement. I'm guessing having him hate me is probably going to suck. But part of me enjoyed it, it was quite the adrenaline rush.

One by one, the others exhale, reminding me that they're in the room with me.

"You must really have a death wish." Kevin jokes. I think it was a joke. I shrug, looking at Shark who is now giving me a look of judgement.

Not long after we were all sitting around the wooden dining table.

"So, Boss, what's the plan?" Evan asks, I can't tell if he's mocking me or not. I pause for a moment, everyone looking at me awaiting an answer.

"Well," I eye the house, "The house could use some work." I say. I stop and think for a moment, looking around the table. "And I'm sure there are other survivors out there that could use our help." I add.

"Where are all those resources coming from?" Ally asks.

I frown, "There are other abandoned houses everywhere, I'm sure there are plenty of usable resources laying around." I respond, my tone more condescending than I intended.

"So, the plan is construction and search and rescue?" Evan asks.

I nod.

"Where's the attack plan?" he asks, narrowing his dark eyes.

"We'll come up with something, but until then let's just do what we know to do. We can clean this place up and help anyone else who might be out there. I feel like if we start there, the rest will come." I look around hoping that the group will agree with me.

"You threw a pretty big fit for somebody who just wants to replace floor boards." Kevin rolls his eyes. I don't know how to reply. He's right, it does seem dramatic of me.

"That wasn't my goal." I say.

"If your goal was to piss off Alec you succeeded." Ally shrugs. "Scarlet, you don't just get to come in here and take over. Especially not on your first day." We sit in silence as I feel my face turning red. After a long moment everyone, but Evan gets up and leaves.

"We don't have to 'come up with something' you know," he says.

"What?" I ask, mostly zoned out.

"You don't have to come up with an attack plan, I already have one." I turn and look at him. I don't have much energy left after today, so instead of replying, I just stare at him. Eventually he too walks out, leaving me to wonder what he meant by that. An attack plan?

After about three hours have passed, I finally built up the courage to talk to Evan alone.

"What do you want?" he grumbles.

"Relax, I wanted to ask you about something you said earlier."

I tell him.

"What is it?"

"You said you had an attack plan, remember? The others may not approve, but in the case where we do find them and we do have a chance to hurt them, I wanna be able to." I explain, "You said something about bombs?"

"You wanna know how to build a bomb?" He doesn't quite buy it.

"Yes, I want to know how to build a bomb."

"Follow me." he says, looking around the living room to make sure it's clear. I follow him to the door and outside.

"Where are we going?" I ask.

"I have some notes in one of the houses over here." he explains. "Plans for a bomb, and some other stuff too." I remember Kat mentioning that Evan would disappear for days. This must be what he's been doing, he's actually working on a bomb. I don't know if I'm impressed or scared.

I follow him up the concrete walk of a house on the corner of the next street over. This house somehow looks like it hasn't been touched by the destruction around us, the blue siding is faded, but still pretty. I follow him through the large wooden door. The house is dark. I can see, but not without effort.

"One second." he says as he begins to go around pulling out random pieces of paper from different hiding spots around the house. "Can never be too careful." he chuckles nervously. It seems uncharacteristic of him to act nervous. I'm not sure how I feel.

"Here we go." he says, placing a decent sized stack of papers on the desk in the corner of the small living room, "These are instructions and some research." He hands me some of the papers. I page through them blindly, not sure of what I was supposed to be looking at.

"Don't worry, I'll explain it." He smiles.

"Are those maps?" I ask him, pointing to two pieces of paper that had strayed slightly from the pile.

"Oh yeah," His voice fills with excitement, "So get this, there's this bunker on the edge of New Mexico. I saw it when I was wandering around out there and I could be wrong, but I think they have something to do with what happened."

"Why?" I ask, confused.

"So, these are the blueprints I've been working on." He shuffles through the papers on the table.

"Why does he have blueprints?" I wonder. But I don't ask. I don't want to set him off.

"But, why do you think they have something to do with this?" I ask again.

"Just a hunch." He shrugs. I know it's more than that, Evan knows something, but I don't ask again.

"You can show me how to make one?" I ask, not sure if I trust it or not.

"I've already started to work on one." He smirks slightly.

"How long have you been working on these?" I ask him. I scan the maps, they're filled with detailed notes and color coded dots. I wonder what they mean.

"I've been here a couple of weeks, I started working on this before I even found my way to Alec." he explains. "Ever since I lost my family in the attacks I've been focused on this."

"How did you know how to do all this in the first place?" I want to ask.

"Look Scarlet, the two of us can pull this off." He presses his index finger against one of the maps, "The others may not be for it, but you can convince them. We don't even need them really, you and I could pull it off." I can't tell if he's being serious or if he's just trying to manipulate me.

I'm reluctant to agree to help him, it does sound like pure insanity after all. He stands across from me, his arms crossed over his chest, awaiting a response.

"I don't know." I finally say. I wasn't prepared for this situation.

"Come on, we have the power to do something, so let's do it." he pleads, "Just think about it, we'd make a good team I think."

I wish I could say I wasn't intrigued. Usually when a crazy man with a thirst for blood asks you to join him in bombing a large group of people, the answer would be to run in the other direction. I just need to do something though. I need a distraction.

"I just don't think—" I pause. I know he's insane, anyone could see it, but what if this isn't just insanity? What if he could actually pull this off.

"I'll just say yes, so I can keep an eye on it." I tell myself.

"Just think about it." he repeats. I don't know why he's so desperate for me to help him with this.

"Alright." I reply. He drops his arms away from his chest. I see his demeanor immediately shift. He's no longer defensive and desperate.

"We need to go back before the others notice both of us are missing." he says. "If they find this stuff, I'm dead. Scarlet, you can't tell anyone about this."

I nod, still afraid of him, afraid of what would happen if I told.

When we return, I go in first. Evan says it would be suspicious of us to go in together. I suppose he's right.

Ally and Kat show me to our room and from that point on, the night is filled with the peaceful bliss of sleep. Something I haven't had the chance to enjoy since the attacks.

* * *

"Okay, so you two." I say, pointing to Kevin and Kat, "I know it's kind of sudden, but I'd like to send you out on a search. Just for the next couple weeks. You'll be out looking for survivors." I tell them.

I know Alec telling me I was in charge was sarcasm, but I'm going to show him that my ideas are gonna work, or at least keep us busy until we figure something better out.

"You're cool with this?" Kat looks at Alec, unconvinced.

"You have three weeks, also if you find supplies bring them back with you. If you're not back within the given time we'll probably assume you're dead." Alec tells them.

"Really?" I mouth to him. He doesn't notice. He stopped paying attention to me after the meeting last night.

"Comforting." Kat mumbles, "What if we don't want to go." She scoots closer to Kevin.

"You don't have to." I say. "But I think this will be really important."

"Come on Kat," Kevin smiles, "it'll be a fun adventure." The two of them exchange a look, she offers him a light smile.

"I guess it won't be too bad..." Kat sighs. "But if you get me killed, you are so dead." she says to Kevin.

"We don't have enough people or resources to search for you, so don't die." Alec says bluntly, cutting off Kat and Kevin's conversation. "The rest of us here will begin...fixing up the house." He rolls his eyes. "Because we're suddenly on an interior design show now." I hear him mutter under his breath.

I smile at both of them, "So, will you do it?" I ask, eager to show Alec that I can get them to do what I ask of them.

"I'm down." Kevin says.

"Sure, I'm always up for some adventure." Kat agrees, I sense sarcasm in her voice but I ignore it. The two of them walk away, probably to explain everything to Ally.

Alec comes closer to me, "If they die I am going to kill you," he threatens.

I sigh, running my fingers through my hair, "You won't have to worry about that." I reply, "If they don't come back, I'll do it for you." I say to his ear as I walk past him to where Kat and Kevin are talking to Ally I hand Kat two fully packed backpacks.

"You're gonna need these. They have water, blankets, food, knives, a map, a compass, and two extra bags for anything you find." I say, "Thank you guys for doing this. Be safe out there."

"Here Kev, catch," Kat says, tossing him one of the backpacks. Kat leans in to give me a hug, "I'll see you in a couple of weeks." she says, her voice muffled.

"See ya." Kevin waves. I watch as the two of them walk out the door. I look at Alec but quickly look away. I was telling the truth. If I get the two of them killed, after knowing them for a day. Alec won't have to kill me. I'll handle it myself. I know that more than anything all of this is just an act of pride, of me wanting to prove myself to Alec, wanting to establish my place in this group of people right away.

After they leave everyone else gets to work on searching for anything we could use to clean up and fix up the house. Alec walks up next to me.

He opens his mouth as though he was going to say something,

but nothing comes out.

"Can I help you?" I finally ask.

"I don't like you," he begins, "You seem to think you know what you're doing, and you don't. But, those two will be fine, so don't worry about them. You're doing okay at organizing everything. There's a small chance you might be an asset." I don't know how to respond. It looked like it was physically painful for him to squeeze those words through his vocal chords.

I stand next to him awkwardly, which seems to be the only thing I ever do around him. Other than spark arguments. One more awkward moment passes. Finally, I turn and practically run away. I didn't look to see his reaction, but I'm assuming it looked a lot like somebody trying to suppress a laugh. If Alec laughs, which I doubt.

"Way to go Scarlet." I say to myself. I feel stupid for being so afraid around Alec. I feel even worse for being so worried about impressing him.

After we have a large pile of scraps. I instruct Alec and Evan to begin measuring the boards. Alec grudgingly agrees to his task. Shark, Ally and I began taking out pieces of old, rotting wood that need replacing.

I'll admit I did purposely give Shark the job that was closer to me, I really want to get to know him. I don't know why. The guy is frustrating with his whole silent thing going on, but I'm almost drawn to be around him. Even though he's probably tired of me hanging around him all of the time.

This has been a lot harder than I pictured it being in my head. Much more time consuming than I thought it would be. Ally and I work close to each other giving us the opportunity to talk a bit more. Around lunch, she asks if I'll help her in the kitchen. I agree, grateful for the break from being on my knees.

"So, how're you doing with all this?" she asks me once we're alone.

"I'm fine." I reply, preoccupied with slicing up a potato.

"Really?" she questions, eyeing the large knife in my hand as I aggressively chop the round vegetable, "You seem stressed."

"I've just been thinking. It feels like all of this is pointless, you know? Like we're all just kind of waiting to die. Like we're distracting ourselves from the truth."

"That's not morbid..." she chuckles, "I think what you're doing is just finding a purpose for being here. I'll be honest, it's helped me feel better about surviving. It's brave. Makes me feel like, unlike that potato," She nods to the mutilated potato on the cutting board, "we will all make it through this." she finishes.

"Well, I may not if I keep pissing off Alec like that." I point out.

"Alec's a hot head, but he'll come around. He's one of those tough on the outside, soft on the inside types of people."

"Maybe." I sigh.

"Trust me. I grew up with him around. I know how he can be. He'll soften up, just give him time." she reassures me, "And stop showing off to earn his approval, run your ideas by him. Show him who you are and include him in decisions. That'll go a long way." She lights the stove and tosses the potatoes into a skillet.

"I'll do my best." I reply as I watch her cook, "I'm not trying to take over anything you know." I say after a minute. I gather my thoughts, hoping that she doesn't already think that's what I want. "I just don't want to sit around like we're just waiting for the end. Having a purpose, a project. It gives me hope that things won't be this way forever."

"I get it." She smiles at me, "Hope is the only thing I'm running on at this point."

"It's really all we have left."

We stand in a gloomy silence, our eyes looking at the floor.

"Anyway, why don't you tell me about your family." She changes the subject.

I agree. We talk about our past as we cook. It seems sad, reminiscing like this. But it feels good to remember them. It feels good to know that I remember them.

After dinner I let everyone have the rest of the night off. Evan and Ally both decide to go to bed and Alec goes back to work replacing floor boards. He told us he doesn't like to waste time on sleep. That seems pretty intense to me, but Alec's pretty intense. I sit down on the couch next to Shark. I stare at the wall across from me. He doesn't talk for a long time.

"I don't want to talk." he finally says.

"Trust me. I know." I reply.

"You're not too bad at this though."

I cock my head slightly in confusion.

"You're a natural leader, I can tell. I just think you need to back off Alec a bit. He's a natural leader too. You guys just need to help each other, work together." I listen thoughtfully to him.

"He's so stubborn though." I argue, although I know that he's right. We should work together.

"And you're impulsive." Shark adds. "You got here yesterday and you're already trying to call the shots. That's cool and all but I would want him backing me up if I were you. He won't support you if you keep picking fights with him." I frown.

"You're right." I admit. "You know a lot about us for someone who's known us for less than a week." I point out. I guess he spends all of his time observing. I've seen him watching Evan closely since I got here. He watches the others too, silently. He doesn't reply. I don't want the conversation to end though. I search my brain for something that could possibly spark another short conversation.

"Was it irrational of me to send Kat and Kevin out there?" I ask him. He sighs deeply. I know I'm getting on his nerves.

"Yes.," he replies, "'it was irrational. I think you were just trying to show Alec that you could do something with your position." I want to argue with him about the Alec part, but I can't. I know the reason I sent them out was so that I could look like I was doing something.

"I could get them killed." I say, not expecting him to comfort, or even reply.

"You could." He shrugs. "You have no idea what's out there."

"What do you mean?" I ask, now paranoid. I imagine Kat being eaten by a lion, wincing slightly at the thought. He gives me a look that says he's not going to answer that. I wander off to bed, wondering what he meant.

"You have no idea what's out there." Echoes through my mind.

I lay awake on my bed, imagining Kevin and Kat dying brutal deaths. I can hear Alec working downstairs so I decide to go downstairs and help. If I can't sleep, I should be doing something useful, something to get my mind off of Kat and Kevin.

I climb down the creaky stairs and without a word, pick up some nails and a hammer and begin to work on a different spot on the floor.

"Can't sleep?" Alec asks, still focused on his task. I ignore him. Out of the corner of my eye, I see him put his tools down and turn to look at me.

"What?" I ask defensively.

"Nothing."

"You looked like you wanted to say something."

"I keep thinking I should apologize to you or something, for being rude or whatever. But then every time I try, I look at you and I get annoyed." he tells me.

"Well, if it makes you feel better you annoy me too." I reply.

"I'll admit I kind of agree with you though, It's good to keep working and doing what we can. Gives us purpose, something to do. The other's seem more hopeful since they haven't been sitting around doing nothing." I'm amazed that he's being the slightest bit nice to me. "But anger practically seeps through your pores. I see it in your eyes, a thirst for revenge, for blood and I don't want you to turn the others into that. You have proven to be extremely persuasive."

"Those people, whoever they are, deserve to die." I argue.

"Maybe. But, they could be in another country or they could already be dead. There's no way for us to know who or where they are. We need to focus on us, on rebuilding to where we can start again. We could build all the houses, we can start more gardens, we can move on without hurting anybody."

"I know. I'm just angry so and all I can think about, all that's getting me through at this point, is the thought that one day I am going to get them back." I tell him.

He pinches his lips together and takes a deep, frustrated breath.

"I can't support you in that."

"I don't need your support." I growl.

"Scarlet...you seem smart and if you're goal wasn't mass murder, I would back you all the way. You're a natural leader. But I don't think killing more people is how we should go about this."

"Maybe not," I think for a moment, "but we have to do something."

"I know, and we will. We'll live." He smiles a bit. "You should get some sleep."

"I'm not tired."

"You are," he argues. "You've been hammering that nail for the past five minutes." He points out.

I sigh and nod, "I'll see you in the morning."

I climb the steps feeling weird about the conversation about my apparent blood lust. I feel better about Alec, less threatened by him. I feel worse about myself. He's right...this isn't the answer, but I don't think this anger is going away anytime soon.

I wake up before everybody else. The golden sunlight is just beginning to shine through the hole in the wall. I try not to make too much noise going down the rickety stairs, realizing that maybe we should've started working on the stairs instead of the floor.

It's probably around five-thirty in the morning, way earlier than my body would like to be functional at. I walk around the living room, seeing how much work Alec did. Which is quite a bit.

I walk out into the garden. The grass is wet with dew, a light breeze floats through the air. I find a nice sunspot and sit in it, feeling the warmth of the morning sun on my face. I think about how the world itself still seems so peaceful, so content even after everything.

The sun is still shining, the plants are still growing, the birds are beginning to fly again. I start to picture what life was like before. It gets harder to remember the longer it's been. I pray that even long into my old age I will still be able to picture my family and my friends, picture the earth before. I sigh and lose myself in thought. In reflection. For hours I sit there, in that sun spot and I allow myself to forget everything and live in the past.

Ally calling me in for breakfast brings me back to reality. After breakfast we get back to work on the floorboards. We finished the hallway and half of the living room.

"Guys," I begin, they all stop and look at me, "can we put this on hold and actually do the stairs?" I ask.

"Please!" Ally laughs. "They're so loud! I always feel like I'm gonna fall through." Everyone laughs a little and nods.

"I'll get everything we'll need." Alec says. I could be wrong but I'm almost certain that I could see him suppressing some laughter.

As we work on the stairs, we talk and learn more about each other. I learned that Ally was really into acting. I like connecting with them and learning more about who they were before the bombings. Although, it's obvious now that none of us will be the person we were before this.

"So Scarlet, what about you?" Ally asks. "What kind of things did you do in D.C.?"

"Well, I love to draw. I spent a lot of time sitting on the bench in my backyard, drawing the birds and the trees and other cliche things like that."

"Do you think it's still there?" Ally asks. "The house?"

I frown, "I hadn't thought about it."

"I feel like if D.C. hadn't been attacked, there would be people here, helping us." Ally mentions.

"So, someone managed to bomb the entire country?" I ask, confused. "Who has the resources for that?"

"You're right though." Shark adds, "There would've been disaster relief teams swarming this side of the country by now."

We continue our discussion well into the morning. I hadn't considered any of this until now, did this happen to all of the States?

"Unless they don't care." Evan points out. The thought is scary, but possible. Before the bombings, the government had started to slowly pull away from the states on this side of the country.

"They have to. It's their country." Alec argues.

"Unless, they're the ones who did it." Evan suggests. A small part of me is worried he's going to tell them about his plans. I doubt he's that stupid. Alec would throw him out for that...or worse.

"Are you dumb?" Ally chuckles uncomfortably. "Why would the US government bomb their own country?"

"Just a theory..." Evan begins, "A couple years ago, there was this debate about whether or not they should limit the amount of children people were allowed to have...obviously that didn't fly, but they did start pushing birth control more. You guys remember that?"

"Go on," Alec says, obviously annoyed, but also curious.

"Say the US population was getting out of control. Food prices went up because the food supply was running low. Gas prices, housing, cars. So, instead of limiting children, they decide to wipe out the population, rebuild." Evan explains. I look at him confused. It makes sense, but it doesn't at the same time.

"If they wipe out the population, how are they planning on 'rebuilding'?" Alec asks, no longer intrigued.

"I don't know man. I bet that's what the bunkers are for. I mean there's no way there's only one." Evan replies. I'm now convinced that Evan's crazy, his conspiracies make it obvious, but I won't lie, it is almost believable. It sounds like something he's been thinking about for years.

"Bunkers?" Ally raises an eyebrow.

"It is too early in the morning for this kind of crap." Shark grumbles. We're all shocked that he spoke at all. I see Alec nod to himself, agreeing with Shark. Evan shoots Shark a glare. The two of them hold each other's gaze. The room is filled with awkward silence until Ally can come up with a way to fill the silence with something comedic.

Evan stands up abruptly and storms out of the room. Shark's eyes follow him as he leaves. I watch Shark for a moment longer. What is up with that guy? Why so mysterious? Why so interested in Evan?

After a small lunch of salad and bread, we work non-stop until dinner; except Ally who is our designated chef. We finish the stairs and return to putting the floor down. We all agree on gardening tomorrow. We work mostly in silence. All of us spend the afternoon in our heads, only muttering a couple words when we need a tool from another person.

Our hands are torn up, some bleeding from random mishaps. Our muscles ache and we're tired, we work as if we don't have all the time in the world to do this, as if we have something else to look forward to. We work so we don't feel helpless, so we at least have something to keep our hands busy.

Every now and then I notice Shark and Evan shooting each other glares. I know Evan's pride is hurt from earlier. He doesn't seem like the type that handles being called out very well. I wonder if he's always been like this, or if it's just the aftermath of the attacks. I move myself closer to where Evan works. Close enough that he can hear me, but hopefully the others can't.

"You come up with that theory yourself?" I ask. Genuinely wondering how he knows what he thinks he knows.

"Something like that." he replies vaguely. I frown thoughtfully, considering all of the things he mentioned at breakfast.

"I know they mentioned that we were close to overpopulation, but I thought they said it was solved." I say.

"They never said how it was solved though." He points out, "Everyone assumed it had something to do with the growing death rate, just from old people getting...old. But nobody actually confirmed it was growing." He looks behind me for a second, stops talking and focuses on the project in front of him. Instinctively I turn around to see Shark staring at the two of us talking.

I shrug, "keep going." I whisper. Maybe it's because I just want somebody to blame, but I'm starting to believe this. It's beginning to make sense to me. He shakes his head.

"We can meet at the house later." he whispers, "He can't be around when we talk."

I nod, even though I'm pretty sure he can't see me and get up quietly. I return to my former spot and continue what I was working on before my curiosity distracted me. I feel Shark's eyes on me now, I don't have to look up to know that he's watching me work.

"So," Alec begins as we're all sitting around the dinner table eating some soup that Ally came up with using whatever she could find. "I think we need to go farther out then this neighborhood and find more supplies."

"Look who's being a team player." Evan mumbles.. Alec shifts his attention to him. The air in the room goes cold for a minute. The rest of us prepare ourselves to witness a murder.

"I wouldn't if I were you." Alec snaps. Evan attempts to remain unfazed, but I see him flinch.

"I agree." I say, trying to redirect before the two of them get into it again. "So maybe we can all go out after dinner. We should have about an hour and a half left of sunlight." I suggest.

Alec nods in agreement.

"Should somebody stay here?" Evan asks.

"Why? Are you afraid some dead guy is gonna break in?" Ally jokes. Nobody laughs. I notice Ally and Evan glaring at each other. Ally has a tendency to follow Alec's lead I've noticed. She looks up to him.

"No, we'll all go." Alec says calmly, the sudden shift in his temperament gives me chills. Shark and I make eye contact. He narrows his eyes slightly, making me uncomfortable. I follow his gaze once again to Evan and then back to me. There's something off about the two of them. I smile at him, he stands and leaves the table quietly.

Everybody grabs a water bottle as we head out to find supplies. We start one street over Shark and Evan go into an ugly yellow house. Alec, Ally and I go into the charred house next to it. Ally goes upstairs while Alec and I search the kitchen. We both hear Ally scream and bolt up the stairs to see what happened.

Alec goes to Ally immediately to comfort her, she's shaking and staring at something. I move closer to see what it is. I gasp when I realize what Ally was looking at. I hear footsteps coming up the stairs, but can't turn around. I'm frozen. There they are. Two charred, lifeless bodies crumpled on the floor. It looks like a young couple. My brain plasters the faces of my parents on them. My heart climbs to my throat as I choke back tears. I squeeze my eyes shut.

"Scarlet." Shark puts a hand on my shoulder. Without thinking I turn and bury my face in his chest. He holds me. I listen as Alec and Evan carry the bodies away. Ally continues sobbing in a corner.

"Gather whatever you think is useful." I order, pushing myself away from Shark and wiping the tears from my face. I didn't mean to cry on him like that. "We don't have long until sundown." I take a deep, shaky breath and begin collecting items that I believe to be useful.

I try not to think about the bodies. I am annoyed with myself for crying. Shark stays close to me as we invade the next house and gather supplies. Though I'm suspicious of him, I feel protected having him near me. Alec finds a bunch of wood and tools in the shed. Ally refuses to go into another house, I don't push her. Evan is looking upstairs for supplies while Shark and I search the kitchen for canned goods and water.

"We should head back." Alec says, hauling two planks of wood through the living room. "The sun's going down and it's going to get cold." I finish packing my bag with supplies and stand up, joining Alec by the door.

"Alec, can you and Evan come back for the rest tomorrow?"

35

I ask. He nods. Evan returns from upstairs with a couple of blankets, I didn't even think to look for those.

When we return to the house we all head straight to bed except Alec and I who both decide to work late.

"You doing okay?" Alec asks as we work side by side.

"Yeah, why?" I reply.

"You just seemed pretty upset after we saw those bodies earlier."

"Yeah." I laugh uncomfortably. "You think I'd be used to seeing that by now."

"I'm not sure anyone should ever get used to seeing that."

"Maybe not." I sigh. "It hasn't bothered me in nearly a month. I haven't cried since the attacks." I tell him. "Not until today. I'm not sure if I was ever even sad about it."

"Sometimes sadness manifests as emptiness you know."

"Maybe that's it." I shrug, "I don't know Alec. I'm not sure I've really cared. All I care about it's staying busy."

"Staying distracted." he corrects. I roll the thought around my mind a little bit. "Scarlet, don't beat yourself up because you don't think you're upset in the way you should be. There's no one way to grieve. You chose to distract yourself, to bury yourself in work, and you need to rest. You need to slow down and feel what you're inevitably going to end up feeling."

Is Alec giving me advice on how to handle my emotions right now?

"That's not the only reason I'm doing this." I reply.

He looks at me, confused, waiting for me to finish my thought.

"I'm doing this because I need hope. I need to feel like what we're doing is going to change something for the better."

He raises an eyebrow, studying me for a moment.

"I was wrong about you. Wasn't I? You aren't all anger." His eyes fill with pity for a second.

"Either way," He snaps out of whatever thought he was just having, "You're going to exhaust yourself if you keep going like this."

"So will you." I remind him that he's up every night with me.

"Maybe so. But you-we, cannot keep going like this." He puts his tools away and stands up. "I'll go to bed if you will."

I put my tools away and nod. I can't promise him that I'll sleep, but I will lay down. He gestures for me to go ahead of him on the stairs. I climb them quietly and slide into the girls room. I do my best not to disturb them as I lay down.

3

Chapter 3

I'm getting anxious about Kat and Kevin. I know it's just been a couple weeks and they'll be back any time now. But I can't help but wonder if they're okay.

I'm sitting in the garden thinking when Ally comes out and sits next to me.

"Hey, can we talk?" she asks.

"Of course." I say to her, smiling.

"So, are you still planning that whole, attack thing?" she asks, "Because I was looking at those bodies yesterday and I was angry, sure. It breaks my heart that so many people had to suffer and die. But, I know you want to and it's all Evan talks about, but I just don't want more people to die." she explains. I'm impressed by her understanding and compassion towards the subject.

"I don't know to be honest, but I agree that nobody else should die." I say, "What's this about Evan talking about it?"

"Oh, he's just always talking about how simple it would be to kill them. Like if we could find the one's responsible, it wouldn't be that hard to return the favor."

I stop before replying, "He hasn't talked to me about it." I lie.

"I don't think he brings it up around Alec either, but he's obsessed. He's so angry and aggressive all of the time."

"Aggressive?"

Ally begins to use examples of times where Evan has lost his temper.

I listen, growing more and more concerned by the minute. I didn't know Evan was this much of a problem, although I feel like I should've guessed.

"You shouldn't be working with him." I warn myself.

Ally leaves after explaining everything and I ask her to send Alec out. I think as I wait for Alec to come outside. For the last few days or however long it's been, I've been daydreaming of getting revenge, but is it really worth it? Is siding with Evan my best call? If anybody would know how to handle this, it's Alec.

"You alright?" Alec asks as he comes to sit next to me.

"I don't know," I half smile. "It's about Evan."

"What about him? You don't trust him?" he asks.

I nod. "Ally told me some things he's been doing and saying."

"What did she say?" he asks.

I tell him everything that she told me, everything that I can remember anyway. He doesn't respond at all, he just listens.

"And... don't hate me." I want to tell him about the maps and blueprints.

"Don't hate you more you mean."

"Okay, fair." I pinch my lips together. "You know, never mind, it's not a big deal." I change my mind, remembering that Alec isn't a big fan of mine. Telling him about Evan and I would make it much worse.

"Fine, I don't wanna know anyway." he huffs. "About Evan, I say we just kick him out."

"Just kick him out?"

"Next time he does something stupid, I will throw him out myself. Literally." He cracks his neck

"Alright." I reply, not sure what else to say at this point. Was that last part supposed to be funny? I can't really tell with Alec.

I sit and think for a long time. I stare at the ground and pick at the grass that is peeking through the dirt.

"Isn't it boring? Sitting out here alone," Evan's voice startles me, "staring at dirt."

"What do you want?" I ask, standing up.

"Just going for a walk." He moves closer.

I stand up.

"I've been wanting to talk to you actually."

"About?" I cross my arms over his chest. I can smell alcohol on his breath as he steps closer to me.

"I need to tell you something." he slurs.

"So tell me."

"Not here," He looks around the garden, "come with me."

"Maybe when you're sober." I reply, trying to step past him. He steps in front of me and grabs my arm.

"Now!" he growls, yanking my arm in the direction of the other house.

"Let go of me." I demand. "You don't need to be so rough."

He keeps leading me as if he can't hear me talking. I feel his grip grow tighter around my wrist as we near the house.

"I already saw all the papers." I remind him, hoping he'll let me go.

"I know, but listen," he begins. "I know you think my theories are crazy and the bomb is crazy. I also know you're having trouble not believing me. Here's another tidbit for ya. These people are guilty, they're all guilty. The ones who detonated the bombs and the ones who bought their spots in the bunkers."

"Evan, do we have to go over this now?"

"Just listen!" he shouts, growing more agitated. He is not fun when he's drunk. "They bought their spots, therefore they knew about the attacks. They knew it would happen and they didn't do anything." I know now that he's lost it. He doesn't know anything about any of this. "This is almost done," he says, rattling the bomb. "We can get our revenge. They're just as responsible as the ones who detonated the bombs."

"He's insane." I think.

"How do you even know that?" I ask.

"It doesn't matter! Scarlet, we can do this, together. If you need motivation to help me, now you have it. Now you know just how guilty, they all are. " He holds the bomb up. I stare at it, searching for a way to say no.

"Nobody else needs to die." I reply.

"They do, they deserve it."

"You don't know that! All of this is some conspiracy you made up. I don't even know if there is a bunker."

"You don't believe me?" He sounds deranged now, completely out of his mind. He looks bigger. "You know Scarlet, I thought you were like me. I thought you were angry," He steps towards me, I back up. "I thought you were on my side. We could've done this together. But you think I'm crazy? Don't you?"

"No. I think you're drunk." I say, my voice as steady as I can

41

make it. He backs me to the door. I subtly search for the handle.

"You just want to spend your time playing fixer upper, you don't have the guts to actually do anything that matters." He's standing over me now, the air in the room grows still as we lock eyes. "This is the only way to stop things from getting worse." He pleads one last time.

"Evan, this is insane. There is no bunker, there's no rich people buying their safety. You made this up."

He grabs my wrist again. I won't flinch. I refuse. I continue to hold his gaze, hoping I look unfazed by him.

"If you say a word about this to Alec, you're dead." He threatens. He releases his grip finally and waves his hand, signaling for me to leave.

I run.

* * *

I wake up from a short nap on the couch. I don't remember returning to the house. I look around frantically for Evan, fear grips my chest, but slowly releases me as I realize he isn't here. I sit up and Shark and Ally come to sit by me.

"Have you guys seen Evan?" I ask.

"Not in a few hours." Ally replies.

I sigh in relief, "Good." I say. Almost positive that he's gone.

"Why?" Ally asks.

"Should I tell them?" I wonder. Evan's last words echo in my head and as much as I don't want to be afraid of him, I also don't want to wind up dead.

"Scarlet?" Shark places his hand over top of mine. I do my best to hide my surprise as butterflies shove themselves down my throat and into my stomach.

"No reason." I force a smile. His eyes follow mine to the light bruising Evan left on my wrist. Anger flashes across his face for half a second.

"Please don't ask" I think. His eyes tell me he already knows.

"He disappears sometimes, only to reappear days later." Ally tells me. I remember Kat saying something about that the first night I was here.

"You look exhausted." Shark changes the subject. His hand still rests on mine. I wonder if he's even noticed.

"Sleep hasn't really been my friend lately." I reply, rubbing my eyes.

"We should let you go back to sleep." Ally says, standing up and leaving me alone with Shark. He begins to get up, but I stop him.

"Can you stay there actually?" I ask. I'm still shaken up from the Evan stuff and I don't want to be left alone. He gives me a curious look, or maybe judgmental? I can't tell. "Just till I fall asleep." I say. He probably thinks I'm nuts.

He nods and sits back down. We exchange a smile before I curl myself up into a ball and slowly fall asleep.

I wake up for the second time to the sound of Ally setting the table for dinner. I look to see Shark still sitting at the end of the couch. I smile to myself.

"Evening." Ally greets me, peering into the room from the dining room.

"Hey," I say as I sit up. "What's up with him?" I ask, noticing that Evan is passed out on the floor. A short flash of my recent encounter with Evan plays through my head as my eyes find their way to my wrist again. I'm even more relieved that Shark

43

stayed now.

"He refuses to tell me where he's been so I thought a nice nap would help jog his memory." Alec chuckles and cracks his knuckles.

"You didn't." I giggle a little.

"No, I didn't." He smiles. "Evan came in drunk, he passed out there before I could ask him where he's been."

"Drunk?" I repeat, pretending to not know.

"We need to find out where he keeps disappearing to." Ally says. Everyone nods. I consider telling them again, I should tell them, but it scares me.

"Are you hungry?" Ally asks me.

I shake my head, "Actually, I don't feel well," I reply. The stress of the day seems to have stolen my appetite.

"Oh? What's wrong?"

"It's not bad or anything. I just feel a bit sick is all."

"Maybe you're dehydrated," she replies. "Let me get you some water." I watch as she pours water out of a pitcher into a glass and brings it to me. I take a small sip, it does feel good on my throat.

"I think you're still tired. You haven't been sleeping well." Alec says.

"I've been sleeping enough."

"We're worried about you. You probably didn't sleep well out there before we brought you here and you've been working nonstop the past few weeks." Ally says.

"Ally's worried about you." Alec clarifies.

"I appreciate it, but I'm fine." I say. "I just took two naps."

"Alright..." Alec shrugs, probably tired of hearing my voice.

After dinner everybody goes to bed early, but I stay in the living room. Suddenly I hear knocking on the front door.

"Who's there?" I shout through the door.

"It's Kevin." I hear him call from the other side. Excitedly, I open the door.

"You're back!" I say as the door swings open. I hug Kevin. I look at the two new people that are with them. They found someone.

"Ally's upstairs sleeping. Should I go get her?" I ask Kat.

"I'd say let her sleep, but I've been dying to see her." Kat replies. "I'll go."

She rushes up the stairs, but pauses halfway, "Looks like we missed a lot." She scans the stairs and the floor.

"I'll explain in the morning." I say. She nods and continues up the stairs. I can hear the two girls squeal with delight. I look at Kevin, I don't recognize his expression as his eyes follow Kat up the stairs.

"Scarlet this is Reese," he says, pointing to a short brunette girl. I smile at her but she turns away, "and this is Ty," He gestures to a tall, skinny boy.

"Hi," Ty says, extending his hand to me, he seems friendly.

"I'm Scarlet." I say to both of them. "You must be exhausted, why don't you go get some rest and we'll catch up in the morning?" I offer. I smile at Kevin, glad that their mission seems successful.

"Sounds good to me." Kevin says. He explains to our newest guests where we sleep and sends them off alone. "It's great to see you." He smiles, but his expression quickly becomes serious.

"What's wrong?" I ask.

"It's Kat, some stuff happened." he says. "She had some

kind of mental breakdown."

"What do you mean?"

"I don't know, the night we left it was like something shifted. She was distant. Then...she wouldn't like it if I told you." He stops to think. "Scarlet I don't know what to do. She barely talked the whole way home."

"Well, maybe she was just focused or tired." I suggest.

"I don't think so Scarlet. She's different. She's not as cheerful. She's been extremely cynical actually."

"I'm sure it's just the exhaustion from your trip." I reassure him. "I can try talking to her tomorrow." I offer.

Reluctantly, he nods.

"You should get some sleep."

"Yeah." He rubs the back of his neck. "Okay. Goodnight Scarlet." He walks past me, towards the steps.

I put my hand on his shoulder instinctively. He stops.

"She'll be okay Kevin." I promise. "Give her time." I drop my hand and watch him climb the steps. My hope for the situation quickly disappears once he's out of sight.

"They'll be okay." I whisper to myself. I hope I'm right.

The night was long. I was alone, sitting on the couch, staring at the wall. No Alec to keep me company tonight. I was too tired to sleep, if that makes any sense. I spent most of the time stressing over everything. The attacks, Evan and Alec hating me, my crush on Shark.

Finally, the sun rises in the sky. I watch as the living room becomes golden. Alec comes down the stairs and stops at the bottom, staring at me for a minute.

"Did you sleep at all?" he asks. I shake my head rubbing my eyes. "Scarlet, you should go sleep now then."

I look at him, my eyes burning.

"I should but I can't." I reply. "Haven't been able to all night."

"Why not?" Shark asks.

"Kat and Kevin returned last night..." I say, "but something's wrong with Kat I guess."

"Is she hurt?" Alec asks.

"No, not physically." I reply.

Alec lets out a relieved sigh.

"I shouldn't have made them do that, we could've waited and all gone together." I say looking at Shark who's standing behind Alec on the steps. "Anyway, I'm gonna let them sleep longer, but I need to talk to Kat after she gets up."

"You need sleep too." Alec says. He actually seems concerned.

"No, I'll be fine." I say. I force a smile and push myself up from the couch. I wobble slightly. I hope Alec doesn't notice. "Worry about Kat. I don't need her having a psychotic break."

"We don't need you to have one either." Alec argues. "And that's what's gonna happen. That seems to be what's happening now."

I argue with him until the others come down the stairs and my eyes meet with Evan, and something in me shifts. I'm no longer tired. I'm scared and angry. I want him gone. I feel like I can't breathe for some reason, I grab my chest. Shark raises his eyebrows and begins to open his mouth to say something.

"Okay... I'm not fine. Maybe I am going crazy. I don't know." I say, I'm looking towards Evan but I'm talking more to myself than anyone else. "The world literally came crashing down and now I'm living with a guy who goes by the name of Shark because he won't tell anyone his name and a guy who has genocide on his mind at all times and there's you." I say nodding at Alec. "You're grumpy like all the time, and I get that I came in and stole your show or whatever, but can we get over that please?" I pause, "I'm right there with Kat, just waiting to lose my freaking mind. Cause I'm really scared right now." Tears well up in my eyes as I feel my body begin to shake. My eyes are stuck on Evan at this point. He looks proud watching me spin out.

"I don't think you have to wait much longer." Evan mumbles, probably not expecting me to hear him.

"Now you're telling me I'm the crazy one?" I glare at Evan. "I'm not the one who's-"

He shakes his head, warning me not to say another word.

"Scarlet, you're just tired." Shark says, moving himself in between me and Evan.

"I'm not tired," I whine. "I'm not tired." My voice fades. I'll admit I feel like I'm five-years-old, throwing a temper tantrum. But I can't help it. I can't stop.

Shark and Alec look at each other, completely at a loss.

"I don't know." I mumble, feeling defeated.

"We're all going crazy. Literally everybody just died. I would be worried if you weren't losing it a little." Alec tries to get me to calm down, it doesn't work. I begin to pace. The two of them come further into the living room. I know I'm being irrational, I know I'm not making sense. Seeing Evan did something to me.

"Can you please tell me what the point of this is?" I finally ask. "What's the point?!" I shout.

Shark takes a small step back.

"Am I just going to be this afraid of everything now? Am I just going to keep distracted myself until I can't be distracted

48

from the inevitable anymore? We're all screwed guys. I don't know what to do."

"I...I don't know Scarlet." Shark replies.

"Calm down before you hurt yourself." Alec says. He sounds more annoyed than ever before.

"You're worried I'm gonna hurt myself?" I laugh a bit. "You don't even like me, you don't care if I hurt myself."

"Yeah, I am." He raises one eyebrow. "I'm lost Scarlet, why are you flipping out? What am I missing here?"

Shark turns slightly and looks at Evan and then back at me.

"I don't know guys. I just don't know what I'm feeling. I lost everyone in the attacks, we all did. Shouldn't I be heartbroken? Shouldn't I be depressed?" I back towards a wall, I know I'm being hysterical, I know I'm not making sense, I just...I don't care. "It's like I don't care. I'm angry, that's all I am, angry. I want them to pay. I want them to hurt."

"What are you doing?" Shark asks, stepping towards me.

"I guess I'm just curious if Alec is actually all that concerned about me." I say. I turn and punch the wall with a lot of force. I begin to laugh hysterically, confirming that I've gone nuts. Shark wraps me in his arms while Alec gets an ice pack. Oddly, I feel much better now. My chest remains tight. I feel calm now.

"Seriously?" Shark grumbles.

I shake as he holds me, beginning to sob into his shirt. Alec comes back and presses the ice pack against my knuckles.

"Feel better now?" he asks.

I nod my head.

The three of us just sit there in the corner, my body trembling as Shark holds me. His eyes meet with Evan's who is standing over us now.

"Get out." Shark growls.

"What'd I do?"

Shark rolls my sleeve up, revealing the bruising on my wrist. Alec sees them now for the first time, but waits to see what Shark does next. Shark gently pushes me off of him and grabs Evan's wrist.

"How's that feel?" he asks him, making his grip tighter and tighter. I see the muscles in his forearm bulge slightly. He drags Evan outside. I can hear the two of them arguing about something even through the door, but I can't hear what they're saying.

"The hell was all that about?" Alec asks. I had forgotten he was there.

"Evan's gotta go." I tell him, pushing myself off the floor and quietly walking out the back door.

I keep walking and walking, unable to think. The only thing I can feel is the throbbing of my knuckles as the adrenaline drains out of my system and I'm reminded that I'm injured.

4

Chapter 4

I return a few hours later to a quiet room. Everyone is sitting in the living room staring at me as if they're waiting for me to explode again.

"What?" I ask calmly. I rub my thumb over my knuckles waiting for somebody to reply. Nobody says anything, they look around, pretending like they weren't just staring at me. "Okay, well, I think we should all talk." I say. "Has everyone met Reese and Ty?"

Kevin nods.

"Okay, good." I smile, trying to make everyone feel comfortable with me again. "You guys wanna tell us about your trip?" I ask Kevin and Kat.

"Sure." Kevin replies. He stands up, offering me his seat. I take it gratefully. "So, we left a while ago on a short trip to find survivors, and that's what we did." he began, nodding towards Ty and Reese. "But we didn't just find other survivors. We found information about something else."

I sit up in my seat, noticing everyone else leaning slightly forward, awaiting the next bit of information. "Ty and Reese weren't just hanging around the border between Nevada and New Mexico for the past month." Kevin pauses, "When we met them, they took us to this bunker where we stayed for a few days."

My mouth drops open for a moment. I look around at everyone, watching the shock form and fade on the faces of those who were here when Evan was explaining everything. I watch Evan's face, amazingly his expression stays neutral.

I'm surprised he's still here after the way Shark dragged him out of here earlier.

"There's actually a bunker." I say under my breath. I watch as Shark and Alec look towards Evan. Shark's expression is one I don't know.

"You guys look shocked." Evan chuckles. I knew that was coming. "What an absurd idea." He locks eyes with Alec. I hold my breath, waiting for one of them to tackle the other.

"It is weird to think there might be people just hiding out in a bunker." Alec says, breaking his gaze away from Evan's. I let out a sigh of relief.

"It's fancy Scarlet," Kevin continues, "they've got nice warm meals, soft beds, electricity and running water."

"So, what're we supposed to do with this information?" Ally asks. All of us act as if Evan never told us about the bunker before.

"Nothing right now." Shark replies. I see Evan glaring at him.

"We'll keep doing things how we have been for now." Alec agrees.

"We can discuss it more another time. For now let's get some rest." I dismiss everyone. Everyone breaks off into their own group and begin having private conversations with each other.

"Alec, can we talk in the garden?" I overhear Shark ask. I watch Shark lead him out the back door. The two of them have become close lately. It's interesting watching Shark become more comfortable being a part of the group.

Ty comes over to me

"Hey, how's your hand?" he asks.

"Oh, it's fine. Thanks." I smile at him.

"So you're in charge of all this?" he asks.

"Well kind of but Alec's the real leader here." I reply.

"Eh, I think it may be a bit of a team effort. I was sure you were the leader last night." he says.

"Really?" I laugh. I don't feel like one. I feel like a lunatic.

"Yeah. I mean I've been here for less than a day, but so far it looks like you two are good co-captains." He runs his hand through his dark hair "And apparently you throw a good punch." he laughs looking to the dent I put in the wall.

"Yeah, but it hurt so bad!" I say, starting to giggle. "Alec actually hates me. Stick around and you'll learn all this stuff."

"Alec doesn't hate you." he chuckles a little.

"Just wait and see." I warn him.

He offers a witty response and soon we're both laughing, Ally comes over to see what was so funny. Reese, however, just stands at the back of the room leaning against the wall. I wonder if she's like this all the time, or if she's just shy. I guess that question will be answered in time.

I interrupt Alec and Shark in the garden and immediately they stop talking.

"Hey." I greet them quietly.

"Scarlet." Alec acknowledges me as he walks past me and back into the house. I follow him with my eyes.

"Is something wrong?" I ask looking at Shark.

He avoids looking at me.

"Okay, don't do that." I say.

"What?" He shrugs.

"Don't avoid looking at me like everybody else." I say. "I get it. I lost it a little bit, but like you said I was just tired and stressed out and all this stuff finally caught up to me. But I'm okay, I promise."

He shakes his head, "no you're not."

"Okay, I'm not." I agree. "But none of us are. What happened this morning will probably happen again because we're all tired and sad and scared."

"Yeah, you're right." he says, unable to argue.

"It hasn't been that long you know. I keep thinking it's been six months, maybe even a year, but it hasn't. Two months ago, I was with my parents, in D.C. Now they're not even alive."

Shark doesn't say a word, he just listens.

"It hasn't been that long, but I barely think about it anymore. I don't know if I was ever truly sad." I admit. I run my fingers through my hair. "And I feel like something in me is shifting, there's this fury that wasn't there before. And I'm always somewhere in between wanting to hunt these people down and kill them all and wanting to give up and kill myself."

"There's a lot of that going around." Shark finally speaks "I can't comfort you. We all lost our families and it sucks. There's no good comfort for that. However, the nine of us, while we just met each other, are becoming like family. We look out for each other. We worry about each other. All of us, even Alec, care about you." I'm surprised at how comforting Shark is. I smile at him.

"Thank you." I say somewhat awkwardly. I've never been

good at accepting comfort.

The two of us change our heavy discussion to something lighter, we swap stories about our families. Hard to believe that he was rude and silent, not all that long ago and now he's sitting out here, laughing with me. Now here I am trying not to fall in love with a guy I barely know.

"Did Evan do that to your wrist?" he finally asks. I knew he'd been looking for the right time to bring it up. I look at my hands and back to him. He already knows the answer, if he didn't, he wouldn't have drug Evan out the way he did earlier. I nod.

"You're afraid of him." He studies me. "Did he threaten you?"

I feel protected now. Safe from Evan. I nod again. I can't look at Shark right now. I feel embarrassed. I should never have put myself in that position and now Shark and Alec know just how weak I am. I watch Shark drop his guard slightly as he gently reaches for my hand. Only a couple of seconds after, he pulls away, as if snapping out of a trance. His face hardens and he's back to the mysterious man he was before. As if the last hour of talking and laughing hadn't happened.

I watch him walk back into the house. I feel completely confused.

After sitting for a long time. I grab Kevin and the two of us go on a hunt for water bottles.

"How're you doing?" he asks me. We climb the stone stairs to our first house.

"I've been better." I answer honestly. I find myself squeezing my hand into a fist. It still burns from this morning. "What about you? How're you and Kat holding up?"

This is the real reason I took him with me. To ask about Kat.

"I'm okay." he replies. I watch as he searches through the cupboards. "I don't know about Kat. I'm really worried about her Scarlet. I mean, she's never sad. Well, she never was before. Now it seems like that's all she is." He stops what he's doing, frozen for a moment. I can't help but feel guilty. If I hadn't sent them out there like that, she wouldn't be going through this.

"I'm sure she'll be okay." I tell him. It's a stupid thing to say right now. I don't know she'll be okay. How would I be able to know something like that?

"What if she's not?" He looks over his shoulder at me. "I can't watch her hurt like this."

"I know. It's hard. We just have to hope that she'll pull through."

"There's gotta be somethin' more we can do." he replies. "I can't just sit and hope Scarlet. I have to help her, somehow. Hope isn't enough." He turns back to the cupboard, pulling out a half empty case of bottled water. I feel stupid not knowing what to tell him. I know he's right. Hope may not be enough if we want to help Kat. But, hope is all I know to do right now.

"I don't know." He sighs. "Maybe she just needs some time. I just feel helpless. Ya know?"

"I know. But Kev, you're great at comforting people." I remind him. "If anyone would be able to really help her through this, it'd be you."

"I hope you're right." He carries the water out of the house and heads to the next one. I follow him. Should I keep this conversation going? Was I helpful at all?

"Are you sure you're okay though?" He redirects the conversation once we're inside the other house. "You kinda lost it this morning."

"Don't remind me." I groan. I feel embarrassed about it now. "Yeah, I'm okay."

"If you need to talk." He offers. "I've been told I'm good at comforting people." He laughs lightly. And just like that, the goofy, lighthearted Kevin I know is back.

"Well..." I consider what I'll tell him. "If you really want to know." I find myself venting to Kevin. About everything. Of course I don't go into detail about everything with Evan. But I tell him that he threatened me. It's good to admit that I'm terrified of him. We talk as we walk back to Alec's.

We join the others for dinner. I sit next to Shark. I look around the table and notice that Evan is missing, I think nothing of it since disappearing seems to be his thing. Not long after I notice this, he comes stumbling through the front door. Of course he's drunk again. Why should we expect any different?

Both Alec and I stand from the table and move towards Evan.

"Scarlet," Shark says, gently grabbing my arm. I flinch slightly, he lets go. "Don't. Let Alec handle it."

I ignore him.

"My turn." Alec says. He grabs Evan and drags him up the stairs. I follow.

"Where have you been?" I demand once we're upstairs, even though I know where he was. My hope is that he'll tell Alec where he's been. I don't feel as afraid of him as I did before.

"Nowhere," he replies, glaring at Alec.

"Tell Alec where you've been." I hiss. It's my turn to intimidate. "Come on Evan! Tell him what you're doing." I don't know what's come over me.

"Why don't you just tell him?"

We argue for a few minutes. I look at Alec, who's obviously very confused by the situation.

"He's building a bomb." I tell Alec, "Because he's so hellbent on blowing up that stupid bunker."

"You're doing what?" Alec shouts in disbelief. His eyes shift between Evan and I "A bomb. Really?"

Evan shrugs, grinning.

"These people really are nuts." Alec says to himself.

"I'll show you." I tell Alec.

Before Alec can ask me how I know, Evan jumps on me, pinning me to the ground. Alec tries to wrestle him off of me, but Evan is strong and angry. Evan's fist slams into my face. I can taste blood in my mouth. My head is pounding, but adrenaline takes over and I knee him in the stomach. He doesn't back off.

"I warned you." he whispers in my ear.

"Get. Off. Me!" I cough, trying to wiggle my way free. Alec's still pulling at Evan. I manage to get my arm out from under him and elbow him in the face. He moves his hands to cover his eye and I crawl out from under him. Alec wraps his arms around Evans chest and drags him away from me. But Evan gets enough force to stomp on my leg before Alec knocks him out with one punch.

"Thanks." I say breathlessly. I raise my hand to my mouth, blood drips on my finger.

"This just isn't your day." Alec groans, trying to help me stand. I can't put weight on my leg, he picks me up and carries me back downstairs.

"Ally, get some ice." Alec orders. Ally jumps up from her seat and bolts to the kitchen.

"What are you gonna do?" I ask weakly, wincing as he lays

me on the couch and props up my leg.

"Don't worry about what I'm gonna do." he replies.

"Consider me worried." I reply.

"Where does it hurt?" he asks, redirecting the conversation.

"Everywhere Alec," I would roll my eyes if they didn't hurt so much, "I just got attacked by a very muscular, 200 pound man with anger issues so it hurts everywhere."

He squeezes my ankle gently. I pull back.

"Well, excuse me for trying to help you out." Alec mutters. Ally brings me two bags of ice. She places one on my ankle and hands me one for my head. I feel like I might pass out.

"Kevin, don't let her fall asleep." Alec says as he begins to climb the stairs.

"What are you doing?" Kat asks him.

"I'm probably gonna kill him." he replies, disappearing into the room at the top of the stairs. Shark comes over to me. He sits on the floor next to Kevin but doesn't say anything for a minute.

"Evan?" he asks.

"Evan." I confirm, wincing in pain. "I kinda pissed him off." I admit.

"Shark, you have to stop Alec." Kat says.

Shark stares at her, "Why?"

"Because he's really mad and he might actually kill Evan." Ally replies before Kat can.

"Let him." Shark growls. He holds my hand.

"Shark." I say. He looks at me. "Please." I beg.

Everything goes dark for a minute.

"Okay," he agrees, slowly letting go of my hand, "but only because I want to do it myself." He follows Alec up the stairs. I hear the two of them talking.

Finally, Alec and Shark come downstairs. Immediately everybody stands up and goes to the dining room. Kevin whispers something to them before joining the others. Shark and Alec come over to me. I don't say anything. Shark sits on the floor near my head and Alec kneels next to him.

"Scarlet, I'm sorry." Alec apologizes. I try to turn my head to look at him, but it hurts too much. I want to tell him something reassuring, that it's not his fault. That I'm fine and he doesn't need to worry, but I don't say anything. I listen to his footsteps as he walks away. I reach my hand out to Shark, he takes it.

"That was stupid." he says. "What made you think you could take on Evan?"

"I wasn't planning on him beating me up." I moan. My head throbs with every word.

"What'd you think he was gonna do?" He tries his best not to sound angry. "Why'd he threaten you in the first place?"

"Because I know where he disappears to all the time." Our conversation is interrupted by Alec snapping at somebody in the other room. We listen for more yelling from the dining room.

"He feels guilty you know." Shark says, ignoring the conversation we were just having.

"What?"

"Alec, he thinks it's his fault." he says. I pinch my lips together.

"It's not, this is my fault, I shouldn't have put myself in that position." I reply.

"No. You shouldn't have." he agrees. "But he still feels guilty for not being able to stop it."

"I don't know why he suddenly cares." I groan. "Last I checked, we don't like each other."

"Can you just accept the fact that he feels responsible for you and everyone else in this house?"

"He really feels that bad?" I ask. I can't help but feel some joy knowing that Alec cares about me at all.

"Yeah, he does."

"I'm about to do something stupid." I say, pushing myself up. My impulsiveness takes over as I try to stand up. I start to fall off the couch but Shark catches me.

"You shouldn't be moving." he says, trying to stop me.

"No I shouldn't but I hate staying still. And I'm gonna stop Alec from throwing himself a pity party. Not for something that's all on me." I can hear Shark sigh. It's hard to see, the room feels like a boat. I balance on my right foot and try to hop forward but I almost fall.

"Can you help me?" I ask. He stands there not moving. "Or I could just crawl," I say sarcastically.

"Fine." He wraps an arm around my waist and helps me into the dining room.

"Scarlet, you shouldn't be up," Alec shoots Shark a glare. Shark throws a hand up in frustration.

"He tried to stop me." I say. Ally brings me a chair and Shark helps me sit down. "Alec, you don't get to take responsibility for Evan. None of this is on you. It's my fault this happened." I say. I look around the room slowly, which makes me feel a bit dizzier. "Evan has all these lists and maps and blueprints in a house close to here. He has notes about the government and the bunker, multiple bunkers and a bomb. Last I checked it was almost finished." I tell them. "He's crazy. He threatened me yesterday, he wanted me to help him. I don't know why or with what. But I turned him down. He said that if I told you, he'd kill me."

"I should've known that's what he was doing." Shark mumbles. I can barely hear him.

"You didn't think that would be important for us to know?" Alec asks.

"I don't know." I sigh. "I know I should have told you. I was just scared."

"She's telling us now." Shark points out. Alec grunts.

"After she got herself beat to a pulp." Alec rolls his eyes. "She told us after he almost killed her."

"The man threatened my life." I say quietly. "Like I said, he's crazy, he would've killed me."

"He almost did!" Alec argues

"With you standing right there." Shark growls at Alec.

"Why'd you bring it up up there then?" Alec asks. "If you knew he wanted to hurt you. Why would you piss him off like that?" All three of us are growing frustrated with each other.

"I don't know." I whisper.

"You are not making my life easy Scarlet." Alec closes his eyes and takes a deep breath. Shark abruptly leaves the room, probably to avoid arguing with Alec more.

"I'm sorry." I apologize. "It really isn't your fault you know. I put us both in a bad position." I say once Shark's gone.

"It is." he argues "I should've pulled him off of you sooner. You shouldn't have even been there in the first place."

"It was my choice to be there. And Evan's big and strong and he was angry. Pumped full of adrenaline. I know how hard it was to get him off, I was under him." I say.

"I know...but still." He's run out of arguments.

"Now what should we do about him? He can't stay."

"I have a few ideas." Alec replies.

"As tempting as murder is right now I can't let you do that...

yet." I cut him off. He frowns.

"I won't kill him." He sounds almost disappointed. "But I can't promise Shark won't."

I don't trust that Shark won't either...but I don't want to think about that right now.

"Let's join everyone else in the living room. I need to lie down." I tell him. I feel the energy leaving my body. "And we'll figure something else out when I'm less concussed."

He agrees and carries me back to the couch and gently lays me down.

5

Chapter 5

I slowly open my eyes. Looking at the group of people laying on the floor by me.

"Where's Alec?" I ask, sitting up and scooting my back up against the armrest of the couch. My ankle throbs with hot pain but I try to ignore it. I didn't sleep well because of the pain I was in but I still got more sleep than I did the night before.

"He went to find Shark." Kat replies, she seems to be the only one awake. I look around at everyone in the room. I didn't notice Shark was missing too. I hear the door creek open.

"Scarlet we have a problem." Alec says with the front door partially open.

"What is it?" I ask him.

"Just come here."

I gesture to my ankle. He raises his eyebrows and shrugs.

I sigh, pushing myself off of the couch. Slowly, I hop to the door and lean on the door frame. I look out at him.

"What?" I say, obviously frustrated and in pain.

"It's Evan."

"Is he missing again?"

"No, he's not missing." Alec moves to reveal Evan's body lying in the front yard.

"Is he dead?" I whisper-shout, my eyes growing wide. I can feel Kat staring at me from across the room. Alec nods.

"How?" I ask.

Alec shrugs, "Looks like somebody hit him in the head a few million times and if it wasn't me then I think I have a good idea of who it was."

"He wouldn—oh no."

"What?"

"He's not here." I sigh. "You don't think he would."

"I wouldn't put it past him,"

"Why would he do that?" I lean more into the door frame. I stare at Evan's lifeless body. Should I feel sad? Guilty, maybe? I don't really know. All I really feel is relief, safe. I run my thumb over a cut on the corner of my lip.

"The man is in love with you." Alec tells me "He's only known you a little while, but he definitely cares for you. Of course he's going to kill Evan for threatening your life."

"He's right, Shark loves you." Kat says, I hadn't noticed her coming up behind me. She looks passed me, first at Alec and then at Evan. "Well that's unfortunate." she says unsympathetically. She stares at him for a few more moments. "Shark did that?" she smiles a little bit, but it quickly disappears from her face.

"Yup, I'm pretty sure. Isn't that romantic?." Alec replies sarcastically. "I should probably do something with the body." He looks at the corpse and sighs.

"You think he could kill me next?" Kat laughs, although I can't tell if she's actually joking or not. She's been making jokes like that for the past couple days. Alec stares at her with sad eyes, looking like he wants to say something comforting, maybe scorn her for saying such a thing. Instead he shakes his head and hoists Evan over his shoulder, walking away in a sort of morbid silence.

"Come on, I'll help you back to the couch." Kat offers.

"I have to find Shark." I tell her, ignoring her offer. The others are beginning to stir now, I'm surprised they were able to sleep through all of the excitement.

"You're not about to be wandering around out there with your ankle like this."

"I have to do something." I say "Who knows where he is. What he's thinking or feeling."

"He'll come back when he's ready. Give him time to clear his head."

"When did you get so good at giving advice?" I ask.

"In all honesty, I've just gotten really used to faking being positive." She replies. "Shark could come back. He probably will, but he could be dead out there. He may not come back at all. But even false hope is better than no hope." I look into her eyes, almost as lifeless as Evan's body.

"There's always hope." I reply, completely aware of how cliche it sounds. I wish I knew what was going through her head, how to make it better. But I don't. "

I have to find him." I say "I can walk just fine." I can't...I can barely stand but I have to find Shark. I stand up and do my best to walk without a limp. She doesn't stop me, she's zoned out at this point, staring off into space. I immediately regret walking on it now, as if I had already forgotten what it felt like.

* * *

I walk through the darkness, I'm honestly not sure how long I've been wandering around out here, I've grown used to the throbbing of my ankle. I don't understand how one could be this good at hiding, then again there are about fifty abandoned houses in the area and he could be in any one of them.

What if he's dead? What if he ran away from me? I mean us. Kat's words echo continuously through my head.

I force myself to think of something else, my thoughts shift to Evan. Did he suffer? I almost hope so. Anger flares up in my chest. The words "I'm glad he's dead" float around my brain. I try to silence it but it's no use. I hate him, whether he's dead or alive I will always hate him. The adrenaline drains from my system and I am made aware of the pain again. The endless pain, my head, my ankle, my hand. I sit down on the steps of a house not very far from Alec's. I could walk the rest of the way, but I choose to rest.

"Scarlet?" I hear a familiar voice. "What are you doing out here?" Shark asks coming closer.

"I was looking for you! Where have you been? What happened with Evan?"

He looks down at his hands, still caked with what I'm assuming is Evans blood.

"I'm so sorry Scarlet." His voice breaks a little. "I caught him sneaking out and I started to feel angrier than I've ever been in my entire life and I just couldn't stop myself. I wasn't supposed to kill him. I didn't mean to." He frantically tries to explain. I jump up, wrapping my arms around him. I don't know exactly what I'm feeling, my heart races as I relax into him.

"It's okay." I whisper breathlessly. I feel him shake his head.

67

I pull back and look into his black eyes and smile.

"What?" he asks, searching my eyes for an answer. I remove my arms from around his neck, suddenly feeling shy. I continue to look into his eyes. I don't know what to say next, and then finally it comes to me.

"You make me feel safe." I say. Sure, it's sappy but I don't care. "I know we just met, and for most of the time you barely spoke, I thought you were mute actually. But, I'm just drawn to you and today, seeing Evan like that. It made me feel safe. Maybe it shouldn't, maybe it's psychotic of me to even say something like that. But, I feel safe with you." I ramble.

"I just hated knowing that he hurt you." he replies. I look up and realize just how dark it's become.

"Are you ready to go back?" I ask him.

He nods. Without warning he picks me up. Picking me up seems to be becoming a trend around here. He carries me to the door gently putting me down so I can walk in myself, he hesitates to open the door.

"Go on." I encourage him. He looks at me, takes a deep breath and slowly turns the knob, pushing the door open. The downstairs of the house is empty. Everyone is most likely upstairs asleep.

"We should get some sleep." Shark says. Without argument I hop to the couch, unwilling to brave the steps after wandering around all day long. He lays down on the floor next to me. I can't stop staring at him, I can't help but find it romantic that he killed someone to protect me. I fall asleep thinking that exact thought.

6

Chapter 6

Weeks have passed since Evan's death. The warm summer weather has turned into a crisp fall, leaving us to wonder where our food will come from once winter inevitably strikes. I stopped paying attention to days and months a while ago but if I had to guess we're getting into early-October now.

"Alright, I have a proposition." Shark says, resting his forearms on the coffee table Alec finally allowed us to put in the living room. His eyes are playful which makes me wonder what he might be up to.

"Should I be worried?" I laugh. He smirks slightly, causing me to be more concerned.

"Let's go on a date." he blurts out, the words fly out of his mouth like oxygen after he'd been holding his breath for too long.

"Did I hear you right?" I ask, confused. "You, the vague, brooding man nicknamed after a sea creature that eats people, would like to go on a date?"

"Well if you don't want to I'm sure I can get Alec to go." The two of us have been shamelessly flirting since the night after he killed Evan but I didn't see this coming, not from him.

"Come on, I already got Ally's permission to make some sandwiches and go on a picnic, so we don't have to worry about the kitchen guardian gutting us with a ladle." He jokes. I laugh a bit.

"I don't think you know what a ladle is."

"Not really...but that's not the point. You in?"

"I don't know if we should. We have so much work to do."

"But we don't actually have to do any of it, we have all the time in the world. Let's just go and forget everything for a few hours. Nobody's going to die while we're gone" He pleads. I've never seen him like this. He has been opening up and becoming more loose around everybody lately, but admittedly I miss the mystery.

"You never know. Around here, they might." I argue, but without him having to say anything else I agree. We smile at each other.

"Great, I'll get the basket." He springs up onto his feet and bolts to the dining room.

"Oh you meant right now!" I exclaim, trying not to burst into laughter over his excitement. He never seemed like the type to act like this.

"Yes right now, it's as good a time as any." he replies, walking back into the room with a light brown wicker basket. I stand awkwardly hoping he'll lead the way. He does.

I follow Shark in silence through tall grass and thick trees. A chilly breeze floats through the air, complementing the sun beating down on the world.

"So...where are we going?" I ask, pushing a small branch away from my face.

"You'll see. It's right ahead." he replies. I watch as he steps over a medium sized boulder. I'd hate to admit it to myself, but with every movement he makes and every new thing I learn about him I feel myself begin to fall for him a bit more. It seems sketchy, of course I'd have feelings for the one mysterious guy I meet after everyone else dies. I question my feelings sometimes. Unsure if they're genuine or not, but then he does stuff like this and I just know.

"Here it is." he says pushing through a couple of pine branches to reveal a big clearing. I look around in awe. It's a big open field surrounded by thick trees. I see birds flying around and a couple of squirrels running around collecting for their winter stash of acorns. I haven't seen this many animals in so long...or I haven't been paying attention if they've been around. He unfolds a blanket and lays it out on the grass.

"This is kind of my spot, I come here to think and be alone." he tells me. "There's actually a small stream up that way a bit." He points to a thin path to his right.

"It's amazing." I say, still looking around. I brush the palms of my hands over the grass, it tickles a little. He unpacks the basket, passing me a sandwich. I take it gratefully. "This makes me feel like I should apologize for silently cursing you out on the way here." I chuckle, instantly regretting admitting to that. He gives me an affectionate look, no dark eyes should be able to sparkle like that. I cross my legs as I eat my sandwich. I guess I didn't realize how hungry I was until I had this sandwich in my hands.

"So what's with you suddenly wanting to go on a date?" I wonder.

He shrugs, chewing his sandwich. I wait for him to swallow. "I don't know. I was just thinking, we've been kind of

71

dancing around it since that night and I wanted to take you on a date, forget about everything for a little bit." he replies. He reaches over and grabs my hand.

I finish my sandwich and turn to rest my head in his lap, staring dreamily at the sky.

"This is insane." I sigh.

"What?" he asks.

"A few months ago I lost everything, we all did. The world's looked so dull and grim since then. But, here I am staring at a vibrant blue sky, feeling the cool breeze on my skin, touching the green grass with my hands. It's always been here, through the bombings and everything we've lost." I sit up on my elbow "And it's so beautiful and I think I'm falling in love with it." I finish rambling.

"In love with a field?"

"In love with the field, in love with this life...in love with you, I think." I say impulsively. My heart beats rapidly as I wait for him to reply. I used to make fun of people who were afraid of telling others they love them. What's so dangerous about it? I always wondered. I guess now I know the feeling.

"With me?" he chokes out. "You as in everybody? Or you as in me?" I almost laugh at his confusion.

"I mean you." I reply, breathing in sharply. He stares at me awkwardly for a minute and then looks up at the sky.

"We should probably be heading back soon, we have some work to do." he says.

I frown, I was hoping for something more along the lines of "I love you too" or at least...I don't know, something. I guess this is what makes it so scary. I stand and help him fold the blanket, he avoids looking at me. We hike back through the woods in silence.

Ally meets us at the door when we return. Shark gives me a pathetic look, scratching the back of his head.

"How'd it go?" she asks. She probably picked up on the awkward aura floating around the two of us. I just shake my head and walk past her.

In the garden I find Kat, she's sitting alone, hugging her knees. I consider leaving her to her thoughts, but knowing Kat that probably wouldn't be a good idea. The last few weeks have been filled with Kat's mental breakdowns and pessimism.

"Hey," I say. Walking over to her.

"Oh, hey." she sniffs.

"Can I sit?" I ask, gesturing to the spot next to her.

She nods, barely lifting her head to look at me. I sit down next to her, crossing my legs.

"What's going on?"

She doesn't reply.

I sigh, not sure what to say or do. How does one comfort someone this depressed?

"Kat, you have to talk. Maybe not to me, that's fine. I can get Reese or Kevin?" I offer.

"I don't want to talk." she finally says. "I just want to sit here and be sad." She looks at me for the first time since I came out here. I expected tears but there were none, she doesn't look sad, she looks empty.

I think back to months ago when I first met everyone, Ally and Kat were both unbearably hyper, talking nonstop. Now she barely talks at all.

"Well, I'm just gonna sit here then. In case you change your mind." I tell her. I look over to see her staring off at nothing.

We've been sitting out here in silence for a long time. The sun's beginning to set. I'll admit that I did consider leaving a couple of times, but Shark's inside and that's enough incentive to stay out here. Also Kat needs me. I just wish I knew what to do.

I've seen this type of thing before, back before the bombings. My best friend during Sophomore year became extremely depressed and withdrawn. I didn't know what to do then either. At some point her parents had her admitted to some program in Wisconsin. I haven't seen her since that happened. I felt just as helpless then as I do now.

"Kat, let's go inside." I say. "You should eat something."

"I'm not hungry." she mumbles.

"Just come inside." I push myself off the ground. My legs asleep, my back sore. I stretch. By now the sky has almost become completely black, stars are beginning to peek through the clouds, a quarter moon rises higher and higher in the sky.

"I want to stay out here." she tells me. I don't know what I need to do to convince her to come inside.

"Okay." I reply hesitantly. "But if it starts to get cold, please come in."

"You got it boss." she says, the phrase is supposed to be witty but it just comes out dry.

* * *

"Scarlet, can we talk?" Shark asks as soon as I walk back in the back door. I didn't see where he came from. It's like he was waiting by the door for me to come in, maybe he was. I glare at him, walking straight past. I hear him sigh in frustration.

"What's that about?" Kevin asks me. Him and Ally have

74

probably been discussing our date ever since we got back. I look at him shaking my head.

"Men are stupid." I say.

"Ouch." Kevin laughs lightly.

"Scarlet come on!" Shark calls to me. I squeeze my hands into fists at my side.

"What?" I snap. Turning slowly around to face him.

"Oh boy." I hear Kevin mumble. He backs away from the two of us.

"Can we just talk?" he pleads, his eyes sad. Those stupid, stupid eyes.

I take a deep breath, "Fine."

I walk over to him.

"Let's take a walk." he suggests.

"After you." I say gesturing to the door. I follow him as he walks out of the house.

We walk in awkward silence for a while, alternating who takes a deep breath in, beginning to talk and then chickening out before words can form in our mouths. I realize it's dumb. Being mad because he hasn't fallen in love with me in a month. It's pretty juvenile, but it matters to me. I guess I'm just hoping that I'm not making this up in my head.

"Listen," he begins "I freaked out earlier and I'm sorry. I just...I can't fall in love right now."

"You can't...what? What kind of an excuse is that?"

"I can't go into detail." he sighs. I watch him fight with himself for a couple minutes. "I'm not supposed to."

"Not supposed to?" I step closer to him. I'm not mad. I should be, but I'm not. "Shark what are you talking about?"

"I think I'm falling in love with you too." he says. "I can't tell you everything. But Scarlet...I'm leaving."

"Leaving?" I frown. My heart sinks as I feel myself reach for his hands. "Why?"

"I don't have a reason to stay anymore." he replies vaguely. He's not making any sense.

"Where else is there to go?" I don't understand. "Why can't you stay here?"

"Scarlet, I can't explain it to you." He pauses for a second, thinking of what to say next.

"After everything. After Evan and our date, our late night talks. After I finally give in and fall in love with you. You're just going to leave?"

"I have to."

"No you don't! There's nowhere else to go."

"I have something I have to do."

I glare at him, I don't know how I feel anymore. He stares at me, wishing he could tell me what he's hiding from me.

Then, when I wasn't expecting it, he wraps his arms around me loosely, leans in, and gently kisses my lips.

I freeze, shocked. I'm caught completely off guard, but not disappointed. He pulls away. I smile, wrinkling my nose. The feeling still lingering on my lips like the remnants of some kind of magic. I giggle.

"Did you just kiss me?" I laugh, unable to keep from smiling. "After telling me you're leaving?"

"Yes ma'am I did." He smiles, still gently holding me. I kiss him, more relaxed than last time.

"Interesting timing." I mumble.

"I have to go." he replies. I can tell he doesn't want to. But he must have a reason to go. "Within the next couple of weeks."

"When?"

"Don't worry about that now, we have time." He tells me.

"Can we just be happy for now?" I nod.

I'm still sad, and confused. But I agree to enjoy the time we have now. To be in love, while we still can.

7

Chapter 7

A few more days have passed. Shark and I have grown closer. He hasn't said much else about having to leave, but I know it's still coming. Unless I can convince him not to.

The house is finally mostly fixed up. It looks nice now.

We found some bicycles in a garage nearby and were able to use them to go to a hardware store and bring back some supplies. Carrying everything back was quite a struggle, but we figured it out.

Like we predicted, we're beginning to run low on food as the weather grows colder. We have a meeting this morning to discuss this issue and come up with ideas.

I sit at the dining table waiting as everybody trickles in one by one. Shark and Alec sit on either side of me.

"Morning guys." I start the meeting. "Alright, you all know why we're having a meeting. We're running low on food and need a new plan."

We all exchange glances. Kat raises her hand. I consider not letting her share her idea. I know that it's going to be a depressing, hopeless comment. I nod, signaling her to go ahead.

"Maybe just starve?" she says. I saw that coming. She sees my look and turns away from me. "Or," she begins to make a new suggestion, "we can go to the grocery store and get all of their canned goods and stuff."

"We can, and we should." Alec says "But what happens when that runs out?"

"What if we start hunting?" Shark suggests.

Everyone looks at him like he suggested we eat tree bark... which may at some point be our only option.

"Hunt what?" Alec asks. "When's the last time you saw any animals around here?" Shark and I look at each other, I'm pretty sure I know what he's thinking.

"Yesterday afternoon actually." Shark replies. "There's a stream with plenty of fish in it." I watch Alec's hands grip the sides of his chair.

"You're just telling us about this now?" he asks, his voice calm, but not a good type of calm. I place my hand on his. He looks at me.

"Calm down." I mouth to him. He grunts, turning his gaze back to Shark.

"Okay, I think we should start with fishing." I say. "While the weather's still nice we'll fish and then later as we get into winter let's go to the store and get the canned goods we'll need."

"Yeah, let's just go right now." Alec says, standing up abruptly. "I wanna see this stream." He's obviously upset with Shark. Everybody else follows suit, except me.

"You guys go ahead." I say. They all turn back to look at me. "I'm tired."

"Alright." Alec shrugs. Shark looks at me as if he was asking if I was alright, I smile slightly and nod. I watch as they pack up their gear and head out.

Shark attempts to convince me to come a couple of times. I refuse each time.

* * *

I sit alone, the house eerily quiet. I stare blankly out at the garden, almost wishing I had gone with them. Lately, I feel like my brain has grown to be a dark place. Every time I'm alone, I feel myself growing angrier and angrier. Evan's plans and everything keep resurfacing in my mind.

"*This is what we know.*" I begin to think. "*The bunker is real, so Evan was right about that. What if he was right about everything else too?*"

"The bunker is real." I repeat out loud. A sadistic thought comes over me, like Evan's voice is whispering my ear. I spring into action, grabbing a pen and a notebook.

I write furiously, plotting and sketching. I try to remember the maps and blueprints, as if my memory would be that good. It's not. I never showed Alec the house so all of Evan's stuff should still be there.

"*I'll go look later.*" I tell myself. I no longer feel like I'm in control, my mind races with ideas. I must have lost track of time because before I know it Shark is tapping my shoulder, staring at the papers strewn along the floor in front of me. I snap out of my daze, looking around.

"What's all this?" he asks as he begins to lean over and pick up a piece of notebook paper. I snatch it from his hand and read the top line.

"It's nothing." I say, frantically picking up all of the papers, holding them defensively against my chest. He stares at me confused. I pray that he wasn't able to read any of this.

"Scarlet?" He tries to grab them from me.

"I don't know Shark!" I snap. "I don't know what this is." I take a step back. "I guess I just...had a moment. I was just sitting here thinking and...I don't know."

I lay the papers back down on the floor, face down.

"That's not just a moment." He gestures to the papers. "That's insanity. What happened? You were fine when we left."

"Okay, so now you think I'm crazy...that's great." I sigh. All of it *is* based around Evan's theories.

"Well this isn't exactly sane." he says. "I thought we were past this. I thought you refused to help Evan."

"I don't know. " I say. "I feel like everytime I think I've gotten past it, the urge comes back." I try to explain.

He picks up the list and looks it over.

"So," he starts, I can hear the judgement in his voice, "you're gonna oh, build a bomb!" He narrows his eyes "Because obviously you know how to do that."

"Technically just detonate Evan's bomb." I rub the back of my neck.

"You'll end up blowing yourself up." He chuckles lightly in disbelief.

"You're right. I'll let it go." I say. Hoping that will calm him down. "I'm sorry."

He takes my hands, staring into my eyes.

"Are you actually going to let it go?" he asks. "Don't say that just to avoid conflict."

"No...I mean it. I don't know why I wrote that out anyway." I lie. "I'm sorry." I repeat. He wraps me in his arms.. He kisses me gently on the top of my head, swaying back and forth like he was rocking a baby to sleep.

"Okay, I trust you."

I relax, knowing that at least for this moment I am safe, even from myself.

"You shouldn't." I whisper into his chest.

"What was that?" he asks softly.

"Oh, nothing." I say a bit louder. Suddenly I'm reminded of the night he told me he was leaving. Will this make him?

"Shark?"

"Hm?"

"You're not gonna leave are you?" I know I couldn't handle it if he did. "Because of this?"

"Not because of this. But, I don't know Scarlet." he replies. I'm scared he's still considering it. "I need to go do something... but I want to be here for you."

"I need you here."

"I know." He sighs. "I'm figuring it out."

* * *

Kat walks into the room as Shark picks up the papers, crumpling them up into a ball. She stands beside me so I choose to start a conversation.

"You alright?" I ask.

"It doesn't matter if I am or not. Does it?" She shrugs.

"Kat," I pause, "it does matter."

"Is that all?" she asks. "You just wanna give me a pep talk?"

"No Kat, I want you to honestly tell me what's going on with you...please." I struggle to think of what to say.

"Okay, I feel like starving to death doesn't sound so bad right now." she says, annoyed. "You want honesty? I feel like there's nothing left for me, left for any of us on this earth. Whether there are other people in the world or not, I've lost *my* people and we'll just keep meeting and losing people in this endless cycle. I'm tired of the dead bodies Scarlet. I can't do this anymore." She nearly shouts.

"Not everyone's going to die." I say helplessly.

"Maybe not, but the people I loved the most already did." I can tell she wants the conversation to end. I'm worried she'll walk away and I won't get another chance to cheer her up. To fix her.

"I know you want me to be happy and all that Scarlet." she says to me. "But I don't get how you expect any of us to be happy right now. Or ever again." We stand there side by side for a long moment, not even looking at each other.

"I'm happy for you Scarlet. You're hopeful, dedicated to finding a solution to all of this. But for some of us, most of us probably, hope just isn't enough. There's no fixing this, no fixing me." She scans me silently with her empty eyes before walking away.

I lean against the wall and slide down until I'm sitting,

"What are you doing?" Ty asks, sitting down next to me.

"Thinking." I reply. I stare at the wooden floor.

"About?"

"Kat mostly." I look at him. "I just wish I was able to fix her. To fix all of this."

"Scarlet, processing this much loss is a huge struggle. It's going to Kat a lot of time to heal from this." he says. "But you're doing really well. I know this is hard, but without you keeping us hopeful, we'd all be in the same boat as Kat." I smile at him awkwardly.

83

"Thanks. I'm trying but I feel like I'm starting to lose hope. Alec's clearly been wasted the past two nights and Kat's been suicidal since she got back. It feels like nothing will ever be good again." Tears well up in my eyes. Ty places his hand on my shoulder.

"We'll be okay." Is the last thing he says before I break down in sobs.

The two of us sit in each other's company for a long while after.

* * *

After I talk to Ty, I choose to go for a walk to cool off and clear my head. The air is cool, almost frosty. It's going to be a cold night. I find Alec sitting behind a shed in the backyard of the neighboring house.

"Alec, you alright?" I ask.

He jumps a little. I have a feeling that something is off. I see tears clouding his eyes.

"Alec," I move closer, "What's wrong?" I notice an empty bottle of vodka laying on the ground next to him. "Are you—"

"Go away Scarlet." He slurs.

"I'm not gonna do that Alec." I cautiously step towards him.

"Please, just leave me alone."

I consider leaving like he asks but something tells me not to. I sit on the ground facing him

"Alec, what's going on? Are you drunk?"

"I think that question answers itself." he mumbles, picking up the bottle and chucking it across the yard. "Do you ever question it?" he asks.

"What?"

"Fighting," he says, picking at the grass. "Living out here all alone with literally no reason to do anything."

"All the time. It's been hard these last few weeks." I reply sympathetically.

"Maybe we should stop." he says "I mean what are we even fighting for? Scarlet, there is nothing left to fight for, there's no reason for any of this."

"No, stop," I say, "I can't go through this twice in one day." I mumble

"Just tell me. What is it that we're fighting for?"

"Each other I guess. I don't know. We're family now Alec, we fight for each other." I say. "So...get yourself together and come home because we all need you. We're falling apart and we're not gonna survive this if you fall apart too."

Our eyes meet and I can see how much hurt and anger he has stored up. "Kat really needs you." I add "I just don't know how much more of this I can take." he says.

"You'll just have to deal with it until we figure this out. You'll have to keep fighting Alec, it's your only option." I stand up.

"What's going on with Kat?" he asks.

"Just...come home with me and talk to her." I plead. He just stares blankly at a tree. "Alec, please."

"I'll meet you back there later." he replies. "Don't need them to see me like this."

I nod reluctantly and begin walking towards the house.

I waited up all night for him to return to the house, but he didn't until the next morning and he slept most of the day.

8

Chapter 8

In the past couple of weeks, I've begun to sneak off and study Evan's papers. I've also added my own. I was never any good at this type of stuff in school, understanding it that is. I know I can pull this off though, I have to. I know the others are growing suspicious of me disappearing all the time. But with Alec running off and getting drunk all the time he hasn't been around enough to keep tabs on me. Which means Shark is the only one I need to worry about. I feel myself grow guilty over Evan's death, knowing he wasn't lying. I see Shark's silhouette in the distance, as I'm walking towards the house. I can tell it's him by the way he's walking. He catches up to me fast.

"Hey." I greet him.

"Where have you been all day?" he asks suspiciously.

"Just wandering around." I reply.

"Okay, well we need you back to the house right now, Kat's acting really weird and Alec's missing...again."

I sigh.

"Why can't you handle it?" I ask.

"Because you're better at this than me. I don't know a thing about comforting people."

"Shark, I can't right now. I don't want to deal with it. I get that Kat and Alec are having a rough time, and that sucks, but so am I. I'm tired and I'm pissed off and I do not want to have to comfort everybody else. It's not my job to talk all you psychos off a ledge." I vent. "It's not my job." I repeat, feeling weak and tired.

"Scarlet, I know things are hard for you too, but they need you right now." he says.

"I don't want them to need me." I sigh. But I reluctantly follow him back anyway.

Shark wanders off to find Alec, knowing I couldn't handle dealing with both Kat and Alec today.

"We've lost everything! What's the point Kev?" I hear Kat scream. I stand at the bottom of the stairs and listen.

"I know, Kat. I'm sorry you feel this way, but you've got me and Ally and Scarlet."

"But I lost my family and everything I know." Kat sobs. My heart breaks knowing that she's in so much pain and knowing that it's only going to get worse before it ever gets better. "I shot someone Kev. I killed someone. I can't forgive myself for that."

"You had to Kat. She would have killed you. She would have killed all of us."

"Kat, please just put the gun down. We can talk after you put the gun down." I hear Reese say.

I bolt up the stairs where the voices are coming from.

"Kat, please put it down." Ally says softly, moving cautiously towards Kat. Her outstretched arm trembles.

"I can't do this anymore. It's too much." she cries. "It hurts

87

too much."

"Please Kat." Kevin's voice breaks as he searches for the right words to say to her.

I'm paralyzed, unable to move or speak. Nobody notices that I've entered the room and I'm afraid of what will happen if they do.

"I'm sorry." Kat says. Her body trembles as she adjusts her grip on the loaded pistol. Ty notices me but says nothing to the group of worried teenagers.

"I just want it to stop." Kat whispers.

"Please." Kevin steps towards her. He's almost close enough to reach for the gun. I open my mouth to speak as I see Kat's finger begin to add more pressure to the trigger and then *Bang*. Her body drops to the ground, a pool of blood surrounds her head. Kevin and Ally race to her still warm, but lifeless body. Kevin picks her up and holds her trying to convince her to wake up while Ally cries uncontrollably staring into her friend's dull eyes.

Everything seems to be moving in slow motion. Reese turns away, unable to look. All I see is the smoking gun as a pit of emptiness grows in my stomach. I wasn't here. Kat was hurting and I wasn't here. Guilt creeps up into my throat as I watch the scene play out in front of me. I was so worried about myself. I didn't even want to come. I told Shark I didn't want to deal with this.

Everything was going so well and then this. I slowly walk towards Kat and squat down. Without thinking I grab the gun and stare at it for a second before throwing it out the open window. I run my fingers through my hair.

"I can't believe this." I whisper. Kevin gives Ally a hug and leaves the room.

"Who's gonna tell Alec?" Ally asks, she's holding Kat's pale hand now.

"I'll handle it." I say. I hope Alec doesn't return until he's slept off the vodka I know he's been drinking.

I feel like I might throw up. Guilt finds its place in my chest as I run through every other scenario that didn't end in that gun going off.

I stand up, still in shock. I don't know where my legs are taking me, but I follow them.

"Kevin." I say walking onto the porch.

"I should've done something." he mumbles. He stares at his hands, now covered in blood.

"What were you supposed to do?" I ask, sitting down next to him.

"I should've grabbed the gun or I don't know." His voice cracks and tears begin to roll down his cheeks again. I don't know how to respond to this. I have no idea what to say to make him feel better.

"She was alive this morning." He sobs "She was here and now she's not."

I stare at him. I don't know how to help him. I didn't know how to help her. I feel useless.

"How does that even happen Scarlet?" He looks at me.

"I don't know." I reply, my voice coming out as a strangled whisper.

"How did we get here?" he asks "How did everything go so wrong, so fast?"

"I don't know." I repeat, looking at my shoes.

"You don't know anything do you?" he snaps. "You and your stupid fake positive attitude. You keep saying this will get better, everything will get easier. You promised me she'd be okay. She'd get through this. But she isn't okay, she's dead! Nothing's getting better. Maybe we should all just follow Kat's lead and shoot ourselves in the head."

"Don't say that."

"Why not? It's the truth, there's nothing out here. There's nothing in this world for us. Not anymore. Not if she's gone."

I don't know what to say. Especially since I'm beginning to agree with him.

"It's your fault you know." he says. "You sent us out there to prove a point to Alec, and it wrecked her."

"I didn't mean to." I reply through a shaky breath.

"But you did!" he shouts. I lean away from him, startled. "I'm sorry. I didn't mean to snap at you."

"When we were on our trip." he begins. "When we were on our trip we met a girl, Carrie. She was in the bunker with us. She seemed sweet and Kat got close to her.

One day, Kat overheard Carrie and her husband discussing something. Or she tried to listen in, but she didn't hear what it was about.

They saw her. Kat confronted Carrie about it after. The two of them were fighting about it, like screaming, shouting, eventually shoving, sort of fighting." He pauses for a breath. "Carrie pulled a gun on Kat. Kat managed to get the gun from Carrie and shot her with it. The same pistol she used today. We never learned what it was about, we just ran after it went down. It messed with her a lot though, I could tell. Kat was too sweet, too optimistic to be responsible for taking a life."

"I had no idea." I say. "What were they trying to hide?" I

wonder.

"Don't know, whatever Carrie thought Kat heard must have been a big deal." he responds. "But why does that matter now? Kat is dead. Can you stop living in your made up, conspiracy world, and think about her? Just for a moment?"

"I'm sorry." I cover my mouth with my hand as tears drip on top of it. A wave of anger crashes over me and with all my strength I scream. I hit the wooden porch with the palm of my hand and I scream and I keep screaming until my throat is sore and no noise comes out.

I feel as lifeless as Kat looked, my hands begin to shake as much as hers did as she pulled the trigger. The entire scene plays out in my head as I cry every tear I have and remember that if she hadn't gone on that trip she would still be here.

Kevin's right, it's my fault. All of this is, and I have to fix it somehow. I have to make this right.

"I'll leave you alone." Kevin says after a moment. "I think we could all use some time to process."

"It should have been me." I say numbly.

"What?" He turns back around.

"I should've gone on that trip with you. I shouldn't have sent Kat. I should be the one who's dead, not her. It shouldn't have been her."

I know that he wouldn't say it, but he agrees.

After he leaves, I wait for a few minutes before sneaking off to the other house. I enter the house and begin to pull out all of Evan's stuff. It doesn't seem crazy anymore.

I begin to feel like I got Evan killed for being right. His plans are detailed enough that I think I might know what to do next, maybe. I pull the device out from under the table and begin gently tinkering with different wires and things. He had most of the work done and I'm grateful for that. I read off his checklist and check the bomb three times before realizing the only thing I really have to do is put the outside cover on and get it inside of the bunker.

As I read through his plan, I realize that I only have a vague idea of where the bunker is. Evan has these two maps, but it only has a large circle around where he thought he remembered the bunker being. How do I find it?

My thoughts are interrupted when I hear the door slowly open. Quickly I run around the room, picking up the papers and shoving them under the couch. I hear heavy footsteps coming towards me. I see Alec coming through the doorway, he fixes his eyes on me.

"Scarlet, what are you doing hiding in here?" he asks.

"Just wandering around." I lie. "What are you doing here?"

"We've been looking for you all day." he tells me. "Are you okay?"

"So, you know then?" I ask, making sure before I say anything about Kat's death. He looks away from me.

"Yeah." He takes a deep breath. "I know."

"I'm so sorry Alec. I should've been there. I shouldn't have been—" I stop myself before I say too much. "It's my fault." I finish.

He doesn't disagree.

"What were you doing?" he asks suspiciously. "Why weren't you at the house?"

"I was going for a walk." I lie, again.

"You've been going on a lot of walks."

"I like walks."

"Is that all it is?" He scans the room again. I can tell he

doesn't believe me. "You disappear a lot."

"Yeah, that's it."

"Alright." He frowns "Well, you should come back to the house. We're gonna bury her and I think you need to be there."

"I don't want to." I reply, looking down at the floor. "I don't want to see her like that again."

"Scarlet, come say goodbye. This'll be your only chance." I feel sick to my stomach, the scene plays out in my head once more.

"I can't"

"You'll regret it if you don't." Alec begins to walk out of the house.

"Wait!" I shout after him. "I'll come." I can't let my guilt stop me from saying goodbye.

We walk close to each other. I keep feeling like I should say something comforting or apologize again or something.

"It wasn't your fault." He breaks the silence.

"Feels like it is." I reply. "It feels like there was a string of events that caused it to happen and all of them were set in motion by me."

"Maybe, but in the end it was Kat's choice. I know you tried. I saw how much you worried about her."

"It wasn't enough Alec. We didn't do enough." I begin to cry.

"No...we didn't." he agrees, his eyes falling to the ground. We walk around to the yard beyond the garden where Shark and Kevin are almost finished digging a Kat's grave.

"This is gonna suck." I mumble to Alec.

"Yup, it is." He nods.

We both take a deep breath before joining the others.

9

Chapter 9

As I stare into the hole that the boys have dug, I realize that I'm not overwhelmed by grief now. Sure I'll miss Kat, or I probably will, but all I feel is jealous. Maybe it's messed up, a little sadistic. Maybe she wasn't crazy, maybe she did the right thing for herself. Why should we have to bother with this anymore? Nobody else has to. My mind takes me back to the day I sent them out there. I replay the conversation Alec and I had right after.

"You can't do that until you take care of that bunker." I tell myself. I question why I even came to this when I could be finishing up everything that needs to be done. I could leave tonight if I wanted to. Maybe I should. Finish everything and leave after everyone falls asleep.

I look around at everyone sobbing. Why am I not sobbing? Sure, I've cried, I was upset, but why not now? I see them bring her body out and drop her into the pit in a less than gentle manner. That should upset me, right? Seeing them plop her dead body into her grave. Thoughts run through my head, I look around at the people with me, knowing they are here but feeling completely alone. Feeling empty and numb. I wonder if this is the denial phase that everyone talks about...maybe I'm just pretending it didn't happen, wishing it didn't.

But I know this isn't denial, I know she's gone. This is me knowing I don't have time to grieve, not allowing myself time to grieve. Not until I do what I need to.

Sure, I sent them out on that mission. But it's the people in that bunker who change her, they're the ones that ruined her. They've taken everything from me. Now it's my turn to take everything from them.

Shark comes over to me. We stand side by side, our eyes on the ground.

"Are you doing okay?" he asks.

"I don't think I've decided yet." I reply. "I'm not really sad, just here. Ya know."

"I understand." he says, his hand finds mine.

"Do you?"

"I think so, but do you wanna talk about it?"

"No, it doesn't matter." I sigh.

"It does matter." he argues. "Kat meant a lot to all of us."

"I'm kind of jealous." I admit numbly. "Like on one hand, I feel responsible and I know that was the worst possible way for that to end. I want to go back in time and save her. But on the other hand, I just wish I was dead too. I feel like she did the right thing."

"So...we should all just commit suicide now?" His tone changes.

"That's not what I'm saying."

"It sounds like it. What happened to you Scarlet? When you first got here, you were all about hope. All optimistic and crap.

Now you're all doom, all the time. You're never here and when you are, it doesn't seem like you are. And now, your friend, shoots herself in the head and instead of being upset, you just decided it was a good plan and you wanna do it too?"

"Kat was full of hope too, and look how that ended. Hope isn't everything Shark."

"Since when?" he says quietly, his eyes on the ground. "What's going on with you? Even before today, you've been acting shady. I want to know what's going on." He suddenly begins to yell. The others are startled, but they don't stop to watch.

"So, you're just going to yell at me in the middle of her funeral. Now's not the time."

"Oh, now you care about respecting her. This morning wasn't the time to run off and do whatever the hell you do when you disappear, but you did it anyway."

"Oh my gosh." I exhale.

"I don't want this to happen to you." He points at the grave. "I'm really scared that it will."

"Well, don't be." I snap. "Just don't" I look at him, knowing that I've hurt him.

"Scarlet?" He squeezes my hands.

"You're leaving anyway. Why bother caring about me?"

"Just tell me."

"What?"

"Where do you go?" he asks. "Do I need to be worried about you?"

"No." I shake my head. Although I know that he should be worried. I'm worried about me. "I was just in one of the other houses, hiding from everything. It's nothing to worry about."

"I guess I understand."

Alec calls Shark over to help refill the hole.

"Will you be alright?" He checks before leaving me.

"Yeah, I'll be alright."

"I love you." He smiles at me.

"I know." I force a smile. "I love you too."

I watch as he joins Alec and Kevin and begins to push dirt back into the grave.

After a couple minutes of watching, I make my way back to finish everything up.

I spend my night packing Evans notes and blueprints and maps. Before I know it, the sun is rising in the sky. I frantically pack the bomb into a backpack, crossing my fingers that it does what it's meant to do. I walk quickly towards our house, hoping to make it back before Alec wakes up. I want to avoid the questions and suspicions.

I open the door slowly, trying to not make too much noise, and there he is, standing with his arms crossed over his chest. I feel my heart climb to my throat.

"Where have you been?" he asks. I can hear him attempting to swallow his anger.

"I just..." I got nothing. No excuses. No cover story. I shrug.

"I've been waiting up for you all damn night Scarlet." He practically shouts, "I was so worried you-" He cuts himself off.

"I what? Killed myself?" I readjust the backpack on my shoulders in discomfort. "I'm not Kat, or you. I'm not just going to self destruct like that. I have things to do. I'm not gonna shoot myself."

"After Shark told me what you said to him at the burial. I was just worried about you." He sighs. "I'm worried somebody else is going to snap and you haven't exactly been acting

97

normal. You've been acting really weird actually." He raises his eyebrows.

I practically choke, my heart still stuck in my throat. What will I say if he asks? I have no lies stored up for this anymore, but he can't know. He'll stop me, and I need to do this, for Kat.

"Where..." here it comes "Where have you been?" The dreaded question, so simple, so destructive. "Were you in the house again? What have you been doing?"

I have no answer. I open my mouth, but the words can't make their way out.

"Where have you been!" he shouts, throwing his arms up. Frustration is shown on his face. "You never sleep, you're never here during mealtime, or anytime anymore. You're the one who told us we needed to do all this crap, and you aren't even here."

"Like you are!" I shout back.

"I'm here more than you are." He narrows his eyes. I sigh and reach my hand behind me to the smallest pocket on my backpack. I unzip it slowly and pull out one of Evan's maps.

"This is where that bunker they found is. I think." I tell him, unfolding the map and pointing to the red circle where I'm guessing the bunker is. "I need to see it." I say. "I just feel like there's something there."

"You've been disappearing for weeks because you were studying a map?"

"More or less."

"You left Kat's funeral to study the same map you've been studying for weeks?"

I don't reply.

"What else is in the bag?" He asks. My heart begins to beat faster.

"Just some supplies." I lie.

"Let me see." He orders. I step back. What do I do? He's gonna kill me.

"You don't trust me?"

"I'll trust you when you stop acting like Evan."

Slowly I pull the bag off my shoulders, holding my breath. I hold the bag out and wait for him to take it. I know I've been too suspicious for him to just let this go.

"Scarlet!" Shark calls to me as he comes down the stairs. I'm grateful for the interruption. Although I'm sure he's not very happy with me either.

"What's going on?" He comes all the way into the room. I put the bag back on while Alec is looking towards Shark.

"I just got back from looking for supplies." I tell him, more confident this time than I was when I lied to Alec. "I was going to go look for that bunker."

"Why didn't you just say that?" Alec mumbles. The expression he wears on his face is one of annoyance. Whether he's annoyed with me or Shark I can't tell. He eyeballs the backpack, but doesn't ask to see it again.

"I did." I reply.

"Why do you want to go there?" Shark has now positioned himself between Alec and I.

"I just need to see it." That's the best I can do.

"So let's go then." Alec shrugs. I hope my face doesn't reveal how shocked I am. "I don't want to stay here anyway." His eyes fill with sadness for a moment before he blinks it away.

"Now?" I ask. Kind of hoping we can leave now.

"Sure, let's get everyone up and packed. I want to know what exactly did this to Kat." He growls. Shark looks like he wants to strangle Alec for giving into me that quickly.

"You know guys, I really don't think that's a good idea." Shark says.

Alec and I stare at him.

"I just..." He's trying to find what he wants to say.

"Why not?" I ask.

"I'm just saying, we've been safe here. There's no need to go anywhere else."

"You're the one who wanted to leave." I try not to raise my voice.

"I don't *want* to leave. I had something I needed to do, but in case you didn't notice I stayed. For you." He yells at me.

I look at Alec, who once again is confused by the never ending drama.

"You were planning to leave?" Alec turns his attention to Shark. If I didn't know any better, I'd think he was hurt that Shark didn't tell him.

"I still am." Shark admits.

"Still?" I feel my eyes grow wide in shock.

"What happened to you telling us we should stay here two seconds ago? If you need to go that bad, why don't we just go with you?"

"You can't come." He's trying so hard not to fight right now.

"Why not?"

"When did you people start acting so shady?" I hear Alec mumble but I'm so engaged with Shark it barely registers.

"I'm sorry. I wish I could explain it all but I can't."

There it is again. His wall.

After he says that, he changes. He's not pleading with me anymore. He's shut himself off.

"Shark..." What do I do? What do I say?

"Just let it go Scarlet." he says, his tone flat. A chill crawls up my spine. "I'm leaving."

"Fine. Then so am I." I cross my arms over my chest.

"You can't."

"I'll go get the girls." I ignore him and run up the stairs past the boys.

Ally and Reese are sound asleep, I'm not careful about opening the door.

"Guys, get up." I say, not sure if that will work.

I poke Ally, she moans and rolls over to her other side.

"Get up. We have stuff to do." Her eyes open and she sits up. I try to smile at her.

"Scarlet, why are you waking me up so early?" she grumbles.

"We need to pack up, we're leaving." I tell her. Reese is starting to wake up now too.

"Seriously? Now you want to decide that all of us are going to just leave? Right after Kat died?" I didn't think she'd be upset about it. Why is everyone so mad at me? "You want to forget her because you know it was your fault." She finishes, her eyes are filled with hatred.

"I'm sorry..." I apologize, what else am I supposed to say. Guilt rests in my stomach again. I turn to see Shark standing in the doorway. My face grows hot, and probably very red. I try to get past him to get into the hallway but I can't.

"What? Are you mad at me too?" I ask. I begin to shake.

"No, not about Kat at least." he says, his voice calm. His hands find my shoulders. He steadies me. Somehow his temper has already subsided. He's no longer hardened. I turn to look at Ally and Reese.

"I didn't pull the trigger." I say. My eyes pleading with Ally. "I didn't kill Kat, it was her choice and if I had known that sending her out there would've ended like this, I wouldn't have done it. But I didn't know. I couldn't have known." I'm not sure if I'm talking to Ally or myself now.

Ally stares blankly at me, speechless. Kevin is now standing in the hallway.

"You guys don't have to come." My voice is steady now. "But I'm leaving tomorrow." I finish, squeezing in between the door frame and Shark and escaping into the hall.

Kevin and I make eye contact for half a second. He looks upset, but not with me. Shark follows me down the stairs, I pass Alec, who was probably listening from the bottom step.

"I'm tired of this." I say as I keep walking.

"Would you just stop for a second and tell me what's going on with you?" Shark asks. Already he's back to being himself. How does he do that? How does he care and then just stop caring like that?

"Why are you so sure we need to leave all of the sudden?"

I sigh and stop walking.

"You want to know what's going on with me? In the last few months I have seen more dead people than anyone should ever have to see in their entire life and I lost another person. I lost someone that I loved, again. Kat just killed herself. I need to know why." I vent. "And I don't want you to leave me, not now. I've lost so many people already Shark. I don't understand anything right now and I need you to come with me to this bunker."

"It isn't safe."

"I don't care!" I shout. "I don't need it to be safe, I just need it to be real."

Shark gives me a look of pity. I turn and walk closer to him. I don't think he needs me to tell him how broken I feel right now, like shattered glass covering the floor. He knows. "You'll be okay." he whispers. I begin to cry a little, and then it turns into sobbing and my body becomes jelly. I've gotten too used to this feeling. Too used to feeling sad and exhausted and broken. I look at him.

"And what if I'm not? What if none of us are ever okay again?"

"You will be. We'll make it through this."

"I almost hope we don't." I reply. "I'm gonna go pack."

I leave Shark standing there, frustrated and angry. I've been doing that a lot lately.

10

Chapter 10

The evening passed by quickly, I hardly slept. Today is the day we abandon our safe haven. It's still early, but I want to see it all in case I don't come back. I walk to the field. There are squirrels are playing by the creek. I think about how oblivious they must be to be so cheerful. It's interesting how optimistic the world seems to be when it's so obviously falling apart.

"You alright?" Alec comes up behind me. He startles me a little bit. "I followed you from the house." He admits, scratching the back of his neck.

"Sadder than I thought I would be." I tell him. "This place has grown on me."

"Yeah, but a new adventure would be good for us." He smiles. "We did good with this place, but there's nothing left for us here now."

"We're safe here." I say, I pinch my lips together and think. "But I just need to do this."

"Come on, Ally has breakfast ready. You need to actually eat today."

I glance at the field again and take a deep breath.

"Yeah, I'm coming." I smile, genuinely for once.

"They all hate me ya know." I say as we're walking to the house.

"They don't hate you. They're just grieving." he replies.

"They blame me for Kat." I frown.

"You didn't get Kat killed." he says "They just need to blame somebody for it. They'll get over it." We climb up the stairs to the porch and make our way to the table where it looks like Ally is just starting to serve breakfast. I avoid eye contact with everyone as I sit at the end of the table. I wonder if they've decided to come with me or not. Will they still follow my lead even though they hate me?

Kevin clears his throat as if trying to get somebody's attention, I ignore it.

"Scarlet." He chokes out a whisper. "I'm sorry."

I'm surprised.

"Thanks." I reply. I look at Alec, suspicious that he might have encouraged this. He doesn't notice me looking at him.

"We're gonna come with you to the bunker." he says, his eyes scanning the room, everyone else nods. "We'll follow wherever you go."

"I'm glad to hear it." I smile. "I want you guys by my side." *Even though I'll probably get the rest of us killed.* I think. "We'll head out after lunch I'm thinking. I think I packed everything we'll need last night." I nod to the few bags plopped on the ground by the door.

"Sounds good to me, I'll make some meals to pack." Ally replies. I'm relieved that they seem to have forgiven me. I'm just scared I'll end up getting them hurt.

After breakfast, I choose to go out to Kat's grave.

"Well Kat," I begin, "here we go, a new adventure." I finally feel it. That mourning, that sadness I wasn't sure would ever hit.

"Wish you were coming, you would make it so much brighter." I sniffle "You were always good at making times like these brighter. I'm really sorry. I'm sorry I wasn't here. I'm sorry I couldn't help you." I wrap my arms around myself. I tremble and cry. "I'm gonna fix this Kat. I'm gonna fix it all." I promise. I sit down in the grass by her grave and cry. I didn't think it would hit this hard. I didn't know I'd miss her this much.

"I'm so sorry." I repeat over and over. I just wish I could bring her back and tell her how sorry I am. I wish I could hear her. I wish I could hug her. I feel bad for leaving her here. I don't want to leave her behind, all alone, she hated being alone.

A sudden breeze blows through, rustling the leaves and the flowers. I know it's stupid to believe in signs from people who've died, but if I'm going to get through this I have to believe she was forgiving me. I have to, or I might as well join her down there.

I stand up, wiping my eyes and brushing my pants off. "I might see you soon depending on how this goes." I tell her. "I don't want to leave them, but I have a plan and if it goes how I want. I don't think I'll be here much longer." I frown.

That's the first time I've admitted that to myself. That I could die and the chance is pretty high.

"Why'd you do it Kat?" I sob. "I need you here. You made the days so much more bearable and now I just don't want to be here either. Why couldn't you wait it out?"

I sigh and walk away, leaving my tears at her grave.

I pass Ally as she walks towards the grave, we shoot each

other a pitiful smile. Ally's taking this really hard, she's been quiet ever since. Of course it was just a day ago, but I can tell this will affect her and Kevin more than the rest of us.

I notice Kevin sitting on the front steps of the house I pass him, but then I freeze. I consider whether I should walk away or try to talk to him.

"Hey." I say shyly, I take a small step back in his direction.

"Hey." he replies after a minute. I take that as an invitation to sit beside him.

"You doing alright?" I ask. I know he's not, but I honestly don't know how to start.

He shakes his head, his eyes tearing up again. I wrap my arms around him. I hope it comforts him.

"I'm really sorry." I whisper. He hugs me back.

"Scarlet, it wasn't your fault." he admits. "I shouldn't have made you feel responsible for her death."

"It's okay." I reply.

"It's not okay. I was just so upset." He inhales sharply. "I was in love with her Scarlet. I loved her more than anything." he tells me. I had no idea, I knew they were close. In love? Really?

"I'm really sorry Kevin." I say. Comforting people really isn't my thing. "But we're doing this for her. Going to the bunker, it's for Kat." I tell him. Although I can't tell him why.

"Let's go. I'm done with this place."

"Now?"

"I hate it here." he mumbles as he stands up. His face suddenly hardened, emotionless. I stand up and follow closely behind him.

Alec is standing right inside the door as we walk in. I make eye contact with him as I sling my backpack over my shoulder. He eyes it for a moment, still not fully believing that it's just supplies.

"We're ready." I tell him.

He nods, "I'll get everyone else ready to roll."

* * *

We've been walking out here for hours. The ground is rough on my feet. I've cut myself off from the group. Paranoia of them asking me about what's in my bag has me nervous to be near them. I feel like they can see it, see through the material of my backpack, see the dangerous device I've been sneaking around with for months.

They can't find out, it would be earth shattering. Kat wouldn't be avenged. They wouldn't understand. They'd hate me.

I also didn't really think through the whole, walking around rough terrain with an explosive on my back part. I didn't think through any of this. I feel as though I haven't been in control of it. It's like I wasn't controlling myself, the thoughts weren't my own. I know I'm not being controlled by something else, but I don't feel that way. I feel like I've been on autopilot for months.

I think through all of the scenarios as I walk. Wondering if it will work, if it will detonate when I need it to. Will I have time to run away? I play through a scene in my head where I'm standing there, in the bunker.

The bad guys are closing in, the bomb in my hand. I'm pleading with the others to run away before I set it off. They argue. Shark tries talking to me the way he does when he wants me to chill out. I feel myself begin to shake, I'm terrified.

"Shark please, just go away." I beg "I have to do this. I don't want to hurt you."

He moves closer to me, our bodies close, his hand on mine.

"If you insist on doing this, you're taking me with you." he says, his voice low. I almost feel threatened. Our eyes meet. We stare at each other, waiting for the other one to break. It seems inappropriate to be so attracted to him in this moment, but it's the only positive feeling I'm able to feel right now.

"We do this together or not at all." he says, our eyes still locked.

I sigh. I don't think I can keep living like this, even if it means he lives too. Tears begin to roll down my cheeks.

"I'm so sorry." I sob. Without another thought I set it off. The last thing I hear is his scream before the world goes dark. I gasp, waking myself up from my daydream.

"Hey Scarlet, we're thinking of stopping soon to eat. That okay?" Ally asks, coming up beside me. I shake my head clear.

"Oh yeah, that's a good idea." I chuckle awkwardly. My eyes scan the group looking for Shark, a wave of relief crashes over me. I smile at him. I know it seems desperate, falling for the dark and quiet guy after everything. He's just so perfect. I run off towards him and wrap my arms around him.

"Are you okay?" he whispers, laughing a little as he catches my weight in his arms.

"I love you." I whisper back. I hold onto him with all my strength.

"What?" He pushes me away for a second, long enough to see my face. I blink away tears before he sees them. I think. "You heard me." I tell him, I don't want to repeat myself, it was gushy enough the first time.

I collapse back into his embrace and breathe in his scent, which is mostly sweat now.

"I love you too Scarlet." he replies. My heart leaps.

"I'm glad you came with us." I tell him. "Glad you stayed with me."

His face changes when I say that any normal day I would be suspicious, but I don't read much into it. I find myself wanting to apologize for blowing him up in my daydream, but we're interrupted by Kevin coming up to us and making kissy noises.

We all laugh heartily. For a moment I thought we may be genuinely happy, Shark and I may be at least. But the weight of the secret I've been toting around steals the joy of the moment away when I realize that in the insanity, I handed Ally my bag to hold. I breathe in sharply.

"You okay?" Shark asks as I wiggle out of his embrace. I smile at him, hoping it's convincing.

"Yeah, I'm just really hungry." I tell him.

"Me too." he replies, lightly grabbing my hand and leading me to the rest of the group. I sit down right next to my bag. I feel better now that I'm close enough to it to snatch it away if anyone tries to pick it up.

"Hey Scarlet, can I talk to you?" Reese asks from behind me. Shark and I exchange a look of confusion. I can't remember the last time I talked to Reese. I pinch my lips together, nod and stand up, grabbing the bag and taking it with me.

"What's up?" I ask.

She leads me away from the group, looking over her shoulder to check the distance between us.

"You alright?" I ask. I try to hide my discomfort.

"So..." She begins, rubbing her hands anxiously together. "It's just, I actually stayed in the bunker before. Not for long. I was only there for like a week or something and they're good people." She looks at the ground.

"Okay?" I reply, confused.

She sighs, "I don't know if going there is our safest choice. When I was there with Kat and Kevin, some stuff went down. I'm just worried they won't be very welcoming when they see us ."

I pretend I don't know about what happened with Kat. I know I may be putting them at risk, and I don't really want to. I just have to get there and use the bomb. Somehow I have to pull this off, no matter what.

"So, are you saying we shouldn't go?" I ask, but even after her saying that I have no desire to turn around. "Because we aren't turning around." My voice trembles slightly.

"I'm saying...I don't think it's safe." she says. I bite my lower lip uncomfortably. My eyes find their way back to my group of friends, my family. I should be more concerned about putting them at risk than I am.

Should I tell them to turn back? To go back home. To let me go by myself. They wouldn't, even if I asked. Alec wouldn't let them.

"Yes, I think we should turn around."

"Fine, turn around. Take them with you. I don't care. But I'm still going to see that bunker. I have to."

"You don't have to, you want to because you want answers to what happened to Kat. But, even if you find it there, it's not be worth it. You're going to get us killed."

"It's not just about answers Reese." *Don't tell her Scarlet.*

"Well, what's it about then?" She steps so close to me that I can feel her breath on my face, our eyes locked on each other.

"Nothing." I drop my eyes.

"Look, if this is just some personal issue you're trying to work out, I get it. I do. But let us go home." She gestures to the group who's now staring at us. "They will follow you anywhere, no matter how stupid. They'd follow you straight into Hell if you lead them there, and that's exactly what you're doing. Give them permission to go home."

"You guys can turn around whenever you want. I'm not stopping you." I reply through gritted teeth. "But, if you guys are going to follow me, and good luck convincing Alec and Shark not to. Then we're going to that bunker. I am not going back there." My voice breaks slightly, I try to hide it.

"This is a mistake." She sighs in frustration, stomping off. I look at the group and think. She's right. I know she's right. But how am I supposed to tell them to turn around without me?

After I return to the group, we grab our stuff and continue our journey. I catch Reese staring at me as everyone puts their packs on, waiting to see if I'll give the order to turn around. I don't. This is for Kat. Right?

Do you really have to bring them with you though? I ask myself. It's a question I'm not sure how to answer. I feel like I can't do this alone, but if she's right. What if I'm leading them straight to Hell and they're just following blindly.

I watch her as she leans in and whispers something to Ty. I feel like she's staring at my bag. I feel like everyone is. I shift my position so she can't see it.

We begin walking in what I hope is the direction of the bunker.

I walk closer to the group than before, but I feel further away. I hold Sharks hand as I walk, but I feel like I'm drifting off into a land of worry and doubt.

"Should I tell them to turn around?" I ask myself over and over. No. We are not turning around.

I look at Reese. This one's for Kat, I'm not letting her down again.

"Is it for Kat though?" Yes. For Kat.

"You okay?" Shark asks me.

I nod, not looking towards him.

"Are you sure? You're squeezing my hand pretty tight." he says as he lifts our interlocked hands up so I can see them.

"Sorry." I mumble, releasing his hand from my grip.

"No, it's okay." he replies, tapping his fingers nervously on the outside of his thigh. "You've just been weird since you talked to Reese. You've been weird all day."

"I'm fine." I force a smile.

"You're not. You haven't been in a while. I know that something's going on with you. I just want to help you."

"I'm just sad about Kat and worried about the bunker. I'm sure everyone's dealing with that."

"There's more than that, you've been running off since before all that. Disappearing in the mornings and not coming back until night or even the next day."

"I just needed space."

"From what?" He's beginning to grow impatient.

"No no no, he's gonna think you were avoiding him."

"Reality."

"What are you hiding?" he asks. I want to tell him. I hate lying to him, hiding things from him. But he'll tell Alec and Alec would freak out. They're going to think I'm becoming like Evan. They probably already do.

"You've been holding on to that bag like it's loaded with

113

cash." He's gonna find out. First Alec, now him. How am I supposed to keep this hidden for so long. "I saw how you freaked out when Alec asked about it yesterday."

"What are you trying to say?"

"I don't know..."

"I'm not hiding anything. I just needed a break from everyone because I feel like I'm failing you guys."

He feels guilty. I can tell.

"Okay, I'm sorry." he apologizes. My chest grows tight as I think about how close he was to figuring me out. I can't bring him with me. It's not safe and I'll get caught before I get to do what I need to do. The sound of Sharks scream plays through my mind again.

"Thank you." I sigh, so quiet I'm not sure he heard me. He pulls me into his side. I feel a lump form in my throat. I know what I need to do now, but I don't want to do it. It'll kill him, but it will keep him safe. More importantly, It'll keep them from figuring me out.

Night comes fast. We are worn. We stop out in the middle of nowhere once we can no longer see ahead of ourselves in the dark. Probably not smart, because we also can't see enough to set up camp, but we manage.

I want to leave tonight. While they're asleep.

I lay on the rocky ground right next to Shark, my mind wanders to him. I know deep down that he'll survive without me. Or do I?

I thought Kat would be fine too. I thought we'd be alright, but look at us now. On one hand it seems like they'll be much better off without me, but what if they aren't?

I know that this is what needs to be done though. It has to be the answer. Kat deserves this, we all do.

I wait until the others fall asleep. My eyes have adjusted enough and the moon is full and high in the sky so I'm less worried about finding my way.

I grab the bag and quietly sneak away. My heart sinks.

I pray that Shark doesn't hate me. I pray he doesn't hate himself.

"Should I turn around?" I ask myself. I shake my head. It has to be done. Evan was right, these people deserve it. I have to.

* * *

After an exhausting night and another full day of wandering towards my destination, I finally found it, the bunker. I could see it long before I got close enough to it to see how big it truly was.

I think about the others. I wonder if they're still headed in this general direction.

Did they turn around? They wouldn't turn around, Shark wouldn't allow it.

I'll have to do this fast, they won't be too far behind me. I trudge along, getting close enough to the bunker to see the entrance. Do I just walk in? Do I knock? I walk up to the large metal door, I wonder how they manage to open it. If they ever open it. I stare at it, puzzled, unsure of what to do now. Am I supposed to just walk in and detonate the bomb? My hand finds its way to the side of my backpack, I can feel the bomb bulging slightly. I raise my hand and ball it into a fist. I knock twice...there's no way they heard it. The door is too thick. I walk around the bunker.

"I really thought this one through didn't I?"

"Hello!" I shout. Hoping somebody will hear me, anyone at all. They don't, as far as I know. If they did, they aren't in a hurry to open the door.

"Can anyone hear me?!" I shout louder.

Nothing.

I sigh in frustration and sink to the dusty ground. It's hot. The suns beaming down like it's the middle of July. I cradle my head in my hands. It takes a couple more minutes before the door finally begins to open. The screeching of metal on metal makes my ears ring, but I don't care, I'm finally able to finish this. The inside of the bunker is dark from this angle. I can see the silhouettes of two people; a man and a woman, but I can't make out their features beyond that.

"What do you want?" The man demands, his voice is commanding. He sounds like somebody who would be in charge of this thing. I don't know how to reply. I can't tell them the real reason why I'm here.

"Richard, honey, don't scare the poor girl. Can't you see she's exhausted." The woman pushes the man, who I assume to be her husband, to the side. She comes closer to me, into the light where I can finally see her face.

She isn't what I expected, her features are small, her eyes are gentle, her smile inviting. She reminds me slightly of my mom, gentle and kind. I instantly drop my guard. I was expecting military; army men in uniforms, carrying around rifles.

"Come on in hon, let's get you some water." The woman gently places her small hands on my shoulders and guides me inside the bunker. "I'm Laura and this is my husband Richard. What's your name?" She's now walking slightly in front of me, her husband directly beside her.

"I'm Scarlet." I reply shyly. Before this, when I was thinking over the plan I felt so bold, so prepared. But now that I'm here I don't feel that way.

As we walk down a long, well-lit hallway, I see children playing on an indoor playground on the other side of a large window. I didn't know there were children here, although I guess I should've assumed. Where else would they have gone?

"Well, Scarlet, welcome." Laura replies, her voice is soothing. "Right this way to the cafeteria." She gestures to a large glass door. The word **"Cafeteria"** Is written in big black letters across the center. Richard pulls the door open, holding it for the two of us to go through. I mumble a thank you as I scan the large room.

It looks much like a school cafeteria, but much bigger and much, much cleaner.

There are older couples in the back playing card games, a group of teenagers in the front corner playing a video game on some device I've never seen before.

"There are families here." I whisper to myself, completely shocked. I wasn't aware that so many people had survived the attacks. I grip the strap of my backpack tight as I follow Laura to the drink center set up just to the left of the door. She hands me a cold glass of water.

"So, Scarlet, how long were you out there?" Richard begins a conversation. His eyes scan the sunburn on my shoulders, I think I see him wince slightly at the thought of them. I sip my water for a moment before answering.

"I'm not entirely sure." I tell him. "It's been so long and I haven't really been able to keep track of the time...sir."

"Well, you're welcome to stay here. We built plenty of extra rooms for things like this." He smiles warmly.

"Built?" I question, realizing shortly after that I probably should have kept that question to myself for now.

"Why don't you finish your water, and I'll have Laura show you to your room? How's that sound?" Richard dodges my question. I'm beginning to have mixed feelings about what I planned to do here. It doesn't look like it's full of evil people who would bomb their own country. There are families here, and older couples, children. Just normal people living the best they can. The way the others and I had for the last few months.

"Normal people who built a bunker with extra rooms in it before the attacks." I remind myself.

"Are you alright hon?" Laura's voice draws me out of my thoughts and back to the absurdly clean cafeteria we've been sitting in. I stare blankly at her for a moment while I process her question.

"Yeah." I reply, my voice giving out on me halfway through the word. "I'm just exhausted." I admit.

"Come on, let's get you a change of clothes and some sheets and then you can sleep all you want. It's safe in here. I promise." She smiles. I nod at her, smiling back.

"Rest well." Richard says to me as the two of us rise from our seats at the table and walk back out the large, glass door.

As we walk further down the hallway, I read the labels on each of the glass doors. **"Gym", "School", "Church".** They seem to have a room for everything.

"So, Laura, how long has this place been here?" I ask, hoping to learn more about the bunker. Hoping to find some sort of reason to execute my plan.

"Couple years." she replies. "Some military guys came in and built it. Not sure why, but we sure are lucky they did."

"Yeah, I bet." I mumble as I breathe in the clean scent of

the laundry room. "And you guys just moved in after the bombings?"

"Before, actually. We saw all the reports and my brother, Doctor Fowler, suggested we seek cover in this bunker. He was a part of the team that was building it at the time."

"Where are all the soldiers?" I continue to pry. At this point I'm not sure I could keep myself from asking questions even if I wanted to. All of this sounds completely innocent, but then what were they worried about Kat finding out?

"They're here." she replies. "They're just not in uniform, toting around rifles. We haven't really needed them. There isn't really anyone out there to be afraid of, and the people here are extremely peaceful...for the most part."

"Anyway, here we are." She opens a wooden door leading to a small bedroom and flips the light switch just inside the room, it's been a long time since I've seen artificial light. In the corner of the room is a bed with a folded quilt laying on the edge, the walls are painted a light gray with photos of what life used to be mounted on them.

"Sleep well, Scarlet. I'll be happy to answer any of your questions in the morning." Laura says closing the door before I could reply, leaving me to my lonesome. I sigh, turning in a circle, taking in the whole room. It's cozy. It looks like the rooms we had in our homes before all of this, it looks...normal. Not my normal, not anymore, but the normal that used to be.

I gently lay my bag on the floor and make my bed. I'll have to admit that I am excited to get to sleep in an actual bed again, but a sadness creeps into my heart as I realize, I'll also be sleeping alone.

There won't be any late night talks with Ally or Kat tonight. There won't be any late night talks with Kat ever again, maybe not with Ally either. I lay on my side and cover myself with the quilt, staring at my backpack.

I feel my eyes fill with tears, I have no need to hold them back. Nobody's here to see me cry. I am now completely and utterly alone.

As I lay in silence with nothing but the sound of my shaky breaths to keep me company. I question whether leaving them behind was the right choice. I question whether leaving Alec's was the right choice.

"They'd follow you into Hell if you walked towards it" Reese's voice echoes in my head. I think about the rest of our conversation. If this place is the reason that Kat did what she did, then I want to know what she knew. I want to end this. But I also want my family back and something tells me I can't have both.

I go deeper and deeper into my thoughts until finally I can't wade through the swamp of my memories and fears anymore and sleep takes hold of my body. My eyes drift gently closed and I fade into an effortless and dreamless sleep.

11

Shark

"Come on guys!" I rush to get us all packed. I should have known she'd pull something like this. I should've known she'd run. "We need to catch up to her."

"Shark," Ally puts her hand on my shoulder, "calm down. We'll find her. She'll be fine."

"Yeah, come eat breakfast. We can leave after." Kevin suggests.

"No!" I snap. "We need to leave right now. We don't have time to eat breakfast." Kevin shudders a little, putting the food back in his bag. I can't imagine what Nathan will do to her when she gets there. I can't protect her if I'm not there. I begin to walk away from the others, towards the bunker. Either they'll follow or they won't. I don't care, I have to get to her.

"Shark," Alec comes jogging after me to catch up. The others walk slowly behind. "I know you're worried. I'm with ya on that. But we have to eat. We're no good to her if we don't make it there alive. We have to take care of ourselves."

I stop and look at him. Thinking for a minute. If we waste time, we could be putting her life at risk. But he's right. We need our strength. I look at the group behind us. Exhausted after a restless night. I scratch the back of my head.

"Fine." I finally give in. "Eat quick. We don't have much time to waste." Alec nods gratefully and goes to join the others.

"Come eat Shark." Ally says gently. I hesitate but I am hungry and I know I can't go long on an empty stomach. I smile at Ally, always making sure we're fed and healthy. We eat fast. I don't allow them to waste any time on conversation.

"Okay. Now we can go." Alec says. He takes over the lead. He was always much better at leading than I. I always find myself following, often blindly. "Scarlet probably left late last night. She's smart, she would've gone right after we fell asleep. Let's be fast."

We follow Kevin in the direction of the bunker.

Alec comes up beside me as we walk swiftly, the sun beating down on us from the cloudless sky. Thanks to Scarlet, Alec and I have bonded over worrying about her. We've grown used to monitoring her behaviour, especially the last couple months. She's begun to sneak off. Nobody knows where. She's been secretive and defensive. I shouldn't have fallen asleep last night. I knew she'd do something stupid.

"It's not your fault." Alec says. He always seems to know when I'm beating myself up over her.

"I don't know Alec. I should have seen it coming."

"Maybe, but it was her choice to run off. Even if you were awake, you couldn't have stopped her."

He's right. I never have been able to talk Scarlet out of something. Not when she has her heart set on it. But I could have tried.

"I'm gonna kill her when we find her though." Alec grumbles.

I haven't decided how I'll react when we catch up to her. I guess we'll find out when we get there.

We spend the afternoon in our own worlds, each of us thinking of something. Me, thinking of her. She's all I've thought about since I met her. My memory brings me to her first day at Alec's. I was drawn to her, I don't know exactly what it was. She was bold, passionate. It was something I always wished for in myself. She was unafraid, willing to stand up to Alec on her first day.

I let myself drift back to that day. Back before everything got so complicated.

She'd come into the dining room. A curious look on her face.

"Everyone, this is Scarlet." Kevin introduced her. She was small, her dirty blonde hair in a loose ponytail. I pretended I didn't know she was looking at me. I focused my attention on Evan, he was my mission after all. Watch Evan and report back. Make sure he doesn't share information, make sure he's not planning anything and report back.

Later that day after dinner, she came and sat by me. I had to remind myself why I was there. I wasn't there to get distracted by a girl. I was there to watch Evan and report back, nothing more, nothing less.

I couldn't help but stare. Her eyes were focused on the floor while she thought up what to say.

"Is your name really Shark?" She began. She knew it wasn't, I

had heard Kat tell her earlier. The name Shark was given to me by Kat when I wouldn't introduce myself. I couldn't reveal my name to them, in case Evan had heard of me before then. I wasn't a fan of the name Shark, it seemed stupid to me. But I didn't protest. I looked away from her, I couldn't get caught up in this now. I couldn't let myself get distracted. "Um...Okay, not a talker." I watched her fold her hands and rest them in her lap.

"I'm sorry." I found myself thinking. I didn't want to ignore her, I wanted to get to know her. But my mission.

"I'm from D.C." She didn't give up on the already dead conversation. I found myself amused by her persistence.

"I know." I replied dryly. I watched a sad smile form and fade on her lips. I instantly loved that sad smile.

"Where are you from?" she asked. I couldn't answer that. I couldn't blow my cover. I wanted to keep talking to her. More than anything, but I found myself scooting away. I heard her sigh, frustrated that she couldn't get more. I felt horrible. I watched as she stood and walked away, my heart sitting in my stomach.

Immediately after, I watched as Evan began a conversation with her. I heard most of it, the two of them didn't even remember I was there. He didn't tell her about the bunker, but I sensed that he might. I sensed that he might try to convince her to help with whatever he had been planning. I convinced myself then that it would be in the best interest of my mission, if I got close to her.

"Shark." Alec startles me back to the present. "You good?"

I shake my head clear, "Yeah. I was just thinking."

"About Scarlet?"

"What else?" I shrug. I find myself wanting to go back to that memory. I want to keep remembering those days, before she became distant and defensive.

"We'll catch up to her." He reassures me. I nod, pinching my lips together. I know we'll catch up to her, I'm just worried it will be too late. After Kat and Kevin's mission, Nathan ordered me to keep a close eye on all of them. I found myself watching Scarlet and Evan's interactions more closely. I reported everything back to Nathan. I told him what Evan was planning, I told him that Scarlet was spending a lot of time with Evan. Nathan's smart, he'll figure it out.

"I know we will." I finally answer him after a long moment of thought.

"Hey, what do you think is in that bag of hers?" Alec has been growing suspicious of Scarlet's motives behind wanting to go to the bunker. Ever since Kat's death, even before, she's been obsessed with going there. He's right to be concerned about what she has planned. I want to tell him what I know. That she's been carrying Evan's bomb with her. I couldn't betray her like that though. Alec's a hothead and the two of them are barely to where they don't hate each other. Telling him would reset all of that. I was hoping the two of us being on her about it would make her change her mind. I knew that we wouldn't be able to but I tried, I'll keep trying when we find her.

"I don't know." I answer his question. "Whatever it is, she really doesn't want us to know."

"You think that's why she ran? To keep us from finding out?"

"I think she thinks she's keeping us safe." Scarlet has always had our safety in mind, in her own twisted way. It isn't always right, the way she handles things. But she tries.

"Maybe." Alec chews on that thought. "Think she's gonna do something stupid?"

"Oh, no doubt." Kevin butts into our conversation, squeezing in between us. "Name the last time she didn't do something stupid." I glare at him. This kid has always annoyed me. Sure, he's funny sometimes, but mostly just annoying.

"She doesn't do dumb stuff that often." I reply defensively.

"On her first day she stormed into the garden and demanded that we do as she said. Causing Alec to hate her." He points out.

"Yeah, she did." Alec agrees.

"She was very passionate that day. I wouldn't call that stupid." I roll my eyes.

"My first day there, she punched a wall because she didn't sleep enough." Reese chimes in. "That doesn't seem dramatic to you?"

"Okay...that was kinda—"

"She taunted Evan. Causing him to beat her up." Kevin reminds us.

"Okay, I get it. No, she doesn't make the best decisions when she's emotional." I admit. "But she's not stupid." I'm offended that they even think that about her, though I can't debate it.

"I disagree." Reese mumbles. I inhale sharply. If it wasn't for Alec instinctively grabbing my arm, I would have punched her.

"Alright." He glares at Reese. "That's enough. Let's just stay focused on getting to her."

I grunt, shaking my arm free from Alec. I walk along in silence, trying to ignore the others. I can't afford to get distracted anymore. I have to get to her before Nathan does.

"And here it is." Kevin says proudly as we come up on the bunker. It's been nearly two days since we've seen Scarlet. I just hope she's safe right now. .

"Home sweet home." I mutter sarcastically under my breath.

"What?" Alec asks, confused. I shake my head. We walk up to the large metal door.

"So, do we knock or?" Ally asks, placing her hand on the metal.

"Just wait." Ty pulls her away from the door. We wait about two minutes before we hear the screeching of metal on metal. A sound I haven't heard in a long time. My heart begins to pound as I wonder how I will be greeted. I was supposed to return weeks ago, alone.

Richard greets us, welcoming us inside.

"Is she here?" I ask him quietly. He warns me not to blow my cover. "Scarlet! Where is she?" I say more aggressively.

"Shark, calm down." Ally reaches for my arm, I bat her hand away.

"No! I need to know she's here and safe."

"Shark?" Laura pushes Richard aside. Her voice soothing, as it always is. "Why don't we go somewhere and talk. Find out who it is you're looking for." She knows who I am, but she knows to not be obvious. Laura raised me after my parents sent me to Nathan for training when I was fourteen.

"Our friend Scarlet, she came looking for this bunker." Alec tells her calmly. "We just want to know she's safe."

"She's here." she responds gently, her eyes meeting with mine. Richard places his hand on my shoulder.

"Come Shark, let's go talk." I know that's a signal. Nathan knows I'm here, he wants to talk.

"No!" I yell. "I don't want to go talk. I want to see Scarlet. Right now." I shove Richard away from me. The others back away, startled. "Take me to her. Please."

"Honey, will you take the others to their bunks?" Laura asks

Richard. He nods. I watch as the others reluctantly follow him in the direction of the rooms.

"Finn." Laura says once we're alone, brushing my cheek with her hand. Laura has always been like a mother to me, she's shown me more love than my mom ever did. "Honey, I know you want to see her. But she's resting now, you can see her in the morning." She looks around cautiously.

"Finn, Nathan can't know about her. He can't know you care for her. That will get you both killed." It's been so long since I've heard my name, so long since I've been in this place.

"I know." I frown. A single tear rolling down my cheek. She wipes it away.

"He wants to see you." She begins leading me down the hall towards his office. "When we stopped from hearing you, we thought you'd been compromised. Thought maybe you were dead." Her voice shakes slightly.

"I'm sorry Laura." I apologize. "I was afraid of..." I can't say it, not here. If Nathan learns that I'm in love with Scarlet, she wouldn't be safe.

"I know." She smiles warmly. "I understand. But be careful, Nathan won't be understanding. You know how he can be." She knocks on the white door.

"Come in!" Nathan calls through the door. I take a deep breath, slowly reaching for the handle.

Laura squeezes my shoulder gently before turning in the other direction, leaving me to face him on my own.

Nathan has always scared me. He's deranged, ruthless and unpredictable.

"Doctor." I greet him as I walk sheepishly into his office. I stand still, my arms at my sides until he gestures for me to take a seat.

"Finn. How lovely to have you back." Nathan greets me. An unsettling grin spreads across his face. I prepare myself for a bullet to the head. As I've seen him do to many other soldiers in the past. "And I see you brought a whole...posse with you."

"Yes sir."

"No need to be so formal Finn. I thought you and I were friends. Nearly family."

"Right, sorry Nathan."

"So tell me. Did you lose your watch? Your map maybe? We were expecting you back weeks ago."

"Yes sir, I lost my watch." I lie. "I'm afraid I was delayed by events I could not predict."

"Lucky for you, I had a new one custom made, for my favorite soldier." He reaches into a drawer in his desk and passes me a white watch. I put it on.

"Thank you sir."

He glares at me for a moment. "couldn't predict you said. What kind of things?" I knew he would ask but I wasn't prepared. It was Scarlet that distracted me from my mission.

"Well Nathan." I begin slowly, giving myself time to think. He raises his eyebrows, waiting for a response. "I was compromised by Evan. He learned who I was and..." I pause. *And what Finn? What happened next?*

"And he...attacked you? Kidnapped you? What did he do?"

"He jumped me." I lie. "Broke my watch, messed me up pretty bad. I was late because I was recovering." I hold my breath. Does he buy it?

"Oh my." he says unsympathetically. "But you're alright now?"

I nod, "Yes sir. Much better."

"Good, good." He stands up, coming over to my side of the desk. My heart beats harder now. What is he doing? "None of that explains why you thought it a good idea to lead them into *my* bunker." he hisses. "That doesn't explain why you thought you could bring those three back here!" He raises his voice. I shudder.

"I'm sorry sir." I do my best to keep my voice steady. "They just followed me. I couldn't get them to go back."

"And Evan?"

"Executed."

"And the girl? Scarlet? Evan's little friend. She didn't follow you. She showed up here earlier today, alone."

"I don't know sir." I say, "She disappeared in the night. I didn't know this is where she went."

"You didn't know." he repeats. "Finn, are you being honest with me?"

"Of course sir. I wouldn't lie to you."

"Yeah cause that would be extremely stupid of you." He walks to the door and opens it. I stand and walk towards it. "Next time somebody wants to follow you here. Next time you can't convince them to turn around and go home." I stop walking. He leans into my ear. "Kill them."

I knew that's what he would say. That's always his answer.

"Yes sir." My eyes meet the floor. "I'm sorry." I mumble.

"You'll have breakfast with me tomorrow, we'll go over your next assignment then. Don't be late." I nod. He slams the door behind me. I close my eyes and catch my breath now that I'm alone. Or I thought I was alone. I open my eyes to see Christopher standing before me.

"Finn!" he squeals, leaping on me. I embrace him joyfully. "You're back! I was so worried."

"Yeah kid, I'm back." I smile, lowering him gently to the ground. "But listen, you can't call me Finn. Okay? I'm on an undercover mission for your uncle."

"Oh, okay. What can I call ya then?" He giggles excitedly.

"Shark." I reply dryly, my cheeks growing hot.

"Shark." he repeats, making a judgemental face. He scans me up and down. "Weird, but 'kay."

"You'll get used to it." I chuckle. He grabs my forearm and begins dragging me down the hall.

"Well Shark. Mom says that you gotta stay in the newbie rooms while you're on your mission. She sent me to show you which one." He puffs his chest out in pride.

"Hey." I lower my voice. "The girl, Scarlet who got here yesterday. Can you take me to her room?"

He narrows his eyes, "Scarlet?" He pauses to think. "Girl from yesterday."

"Come on kid. Your mom said she was here."

"She is." He shrugs. "But I can't take ya to her."

"Why not." I raise my voice unexpectedly.

"Mom told me not to. She's the boss ya know." He stops walking and turns to look at me. "Is she your girlfriend?"

I cough uncomfortably. I wasn't expecting that. Although with Chris, I probably should have been.

"No." I lie, I think it's a lie. I don't really know for sure. "She's just...important."

"Yup, she's your girlfriend." He nods. I sigh in frustration. I know he won't take me to her tonight, no matter how much I beg.

"Come on, I'll take ya to your room and tomorrow I'll bring

her to you. Mom never said anything about that." He smirks slightly. I can't help but be proud of him for coming up with a loophole.

"Sounds like a plan kid." I laugh gently. We walk a bit further down the hallway.

"Here." he says, opening a door to one of the rooms. "They already put all your clothes and stuff in there. You need anything else?"

"No Chris. Thank you."

He smiles at me before turning and skipping down the hall, the way that he always has. I walk into my room and close the door. It's been a long time since I've seen a bed. I sit on it as I sink back into my memories. Back to when things were somehow easier. I don't sleep, but I still find myself dreaming about her and how things were before I came back home.

12

Scarlet

It was weird waking up and not being able to see the sun this morning. I had fallen asleep with my light on, but it wasn't the same as waking up with the warmth of the sun on my face. For a moment I had forgotten where I was. I had forgotten that I wasn't going to be waking up on the hardwood floor of a bedroom in an old rickety house anymore.

That same sadness from the night before attempts to creep in yet again, but I manage to swallow it as I climb out of bed. My feet hit the warm, carpeted floor.

I walk into the bathroom connected to my room. It's already fully stocked with soap and towels. A vase of fake flowers rests on the extra counter space connected to the sink.

"This is a real fancy bunker." I say to myself, as I turn on the faucet, amazed by the running water. It's been so long since I've seen a working faucet. Funny how the things that were normal before, seem so abnormal now.

I return to the bedroom walking around, touching everything. It almost doesn't seem real, seems too good to be true.

An oak dresser is up against the wall across from the bed. I find myself staring at the photograph above it. It's a picture of a young girl playing jump rope with her friends at school. I can't tell if the image makes me feel happy or sad, but it's making me feel something.

As I'm pulling my hair back into a ponytail, I hear a light knock on the door. I freeze for a moment, not sure if that's even what I heard, but it comes again, slightly louder than before.

I cross the floor and open it a crack, not sure what kinds of people live here. My gaze falls on a young boy, probably around age ten or so.

"Hello." I greet him, my voice higher pitched than I meant for it to be.

"Hello." He smiles. "My mom told me to come tell you they're serving breakfast now." He informs me. His smile is infectious or maybe I'm just relieved to know that some children survived, either way I feel a smile spreading across my face.

"Your mom?" I ask.

"Laura." he clarifies. "Come on, we can walk down there together." I join him out in the hallway and quietly close the door behind me. The digital clock in the hall reads **8:00 a.m.**

"My name's Christopher." He introduces himself as we walk swiftly towards the cafeteria. "If we hurry, they'll still have a few chocolate chip muffins left, those go fast 'round here." He chuckles lightly.

"That sounds good." I reply. My mouth waters at the idea of having a real breakfast. I just wish I could be sharing this with the others. They deserve to have a nice warm breakfast for once, probably more than I do.

"I'm Scarlet." I tell him after realizing I'd forgotten to

introduce myself.

"I know." he says, still smiling. "My mom told me."

"Ah, of course." I reply quietly.

"Here we are." Christopher says as he struggles to open the door to the large dining area. I lift my hand to help him, but he just shakes his head. "My dad says I always gotta hold the door for ladies." he states, still struggling to keep the door open.

"Well, he's right, that is the polite thing to do." I reply as I quickly walk through the door so he can finally let go. I watch as he lets the door fall closed and shakes his arms out, laughing shyly.

"Come on Scarlet, the line starts here." The two of us join the line of people at the counter. He passes me a ceramic plate. "Today's pancake day." He beams. "So you'll go up, serve your pancake, get your syrup, get your muffin if ya want it. There's some strawberries and stuff at the end if ya want 'em." He cringes as he says "strawberries". "Get whatever you want and if you're still hungry, after they ring the bell you can go get more."

"Sounds good. Thanks kid." I reply, serving myself two pancakes and moving up in the line.

"My parents always sit back there." He nods to the back right corner of the room.

"Come on, they'll be here any minute." I follow the small boy through the tables and to the back right corner. The two of us sit quietly and eat until his parents join us.

"Good morning Scarlet." Laura greets me. "How'd you sleep?"

"Better than I have in a long time." I reply.

"We're so glad to hear that!" She smiles warmly. Christopher and her have the same infectious smile.

"So, after breakfast, I was thinking that Christopher could give you a tour and then maybe you could meet my brother. How does that sound?" she suggests.

"That sounds great." I reply as I cut my pancakes into smaller, bite sized pieces.

"Here." Christopher leans in to whisper to me. "I gotcha one." He passes me a chocolate chip muffin. I take it gratefully, although I'm not sure I could eat a muffin after finishing off these pancakes.

"Thanks kid." I whisper back. His parents both raise their eyebrows simultaneously, but quickly return their attention to their pancakes.

"You have to try it." he tells me, his eyes focused solely on the muffin in my hand. I break off a piece of the muffin and shove it in my mouth. The kid's right, it is pretty good.

"That stuffs the best, I'm tellin' ya."

"It is good." I laugh a little. "Where does all this food come from?"

"Well, a lot of it was already here and a lot of it came from the remaining stores around here." Richard explains.

"What happens when it runs out?" I ask "There's a lot of people to feed, I don't imagine it'll last forever."

"Lucky for us Dr. Fowler is working on a high-tech solution for that. A solution that I wouldn't know how to explain correctly unfortunately. But you can ask him when you meet him later today." Richard tells me. I guess that's the best I'll get for now.

"Uncle Nathan's the best! You're gonna love him." Christopher chimes in eagerly. His childlike joy is refreshing.

"I can't wait to meet him." I reply, smiling. We eat the rest of our meal in a comfortable silence.

I feel like I did when I woke up at Alec's, confused, lost. Not quite as bold though. No, that's been drained out of my veins. I am not brave anymore. I'm not even sure who that girl who went up against Alec's authority was. She cost us everything, though, that's for sure. I'm not her anymore.

In just one night that girl has disappeared and in her place is a girl who's scared out of her mind. A girl with a bomb lying on the floor of her bedroom, a bomb that she doesn't have the courage to detonate. A bomb that she now has no idea what to do with.

I wonder when the others will find their way here, or if they already did.

I find myself scanning the crowd for them.

"Your friends got here late last night if that's who you're looking for." Laura says as if responding to my thoughts. I look at her in shock. "I don't think they'll be up for quite a while. That, big, dark guy, Shark? He was pretty riled up. He seemed exhausted."

"Oh." Guilt sits in my stomach and what was left of my appetite is now gone.

"We can take you to his room if you want." She offers.

"No, I'm sure he could use his sleep." I shake my head, my eyes finding the floor. I swallow hard, wishing this guilt I'm feeling would go away. I'm tired of feeling guilty all the time.

"I'll clear your plate this time." Christopher butts in, "But you'll have to do it yourself after this." He puts on a fake serious tone, obviously trying to lighten the mood. It may have worked too, if it wasn't muffled by the thoughts running laps around my brain right now.

"I'm sure he won't mind." Laura tries to insist. "He was hell-bent on seeing you last night. We thought we were gonna have to sedate him."

"Oh lord." I mumble "No, let him sleep." I won't say it out loud, but I'm afraid of how both Shark and Alec are going to react when they see me. I know for sure they won't be happy. I wish I had done what I came here to do before they got here.

I'd rather be dead than have to explain this one to them.

"Come on Scarlet! Let me show you around." Christopher says, grabbing my hand and pulling me out of my seat. Laura flashes me an apologetic yet amused smile as he pulls me off towards the door.

"So this is the gym." Christopher says, leading me into the first room. It's a huge room filled with exercise equipment, just like what you would've seen before all of this happened. It was a clean, mostly white room, just like the rest of the bunker was.

"The adults spend a lot of time in here, not sure why, seems kinda boring to me, but 'kay." He shrugs his shoulders in genuine confusion. I find myself holding back a laugh.

"Let me show you the school." he says. He uses his back to push open the door, anchoring his feet on the floor so the weight doesn't crush his small frame. I reach out to help, but am yet again discouraged from doing so.

"This is where me and the other thirty kids do school." he says as we walk into yet another absurdly clean, white room. It looks like a classroom, white board and everything.

"Thirty kids?"

"Yeah, but that's not counting the nine babies and thirteen teenagers. The babies don't go to school and the teens have their own room." he explains.

"How many people are there total? Do you know?" I ask him, knowing he probably has no clue.

"You'd have to ask Uncle Nathan." He shrugs, leading me out of the classroom and down the hall. The bunker is gigantic, full of rooms. I wonder how long it took to build and engineer this whole thing. It took the two of us about three hours to finish the whole tour and the kid talked the whole time. I didn't mind though, he's funny and I enjoyed the company.

"I bet your friends are up." He tells me as we're walking back towards the bedrooms. "We can knock on your boyfriend's door if ya want." I pause for a second, choking on my breath.

"My who?" I swallow uncomfortably.

"Your boyfriend." he replies.

"How do you?" I'm holding back yet another laugh.

"My dad told me that nobody gets as worked up over a woman than a man who's in love with her." He states matter-of-factly.

"Your dad told you that?" I raise an eyebrow.

"Yup, last night when your boyfriend was going nuts."

"Ah, gotcha. Your dad tell you anything else?" I ask, amused by our conversation.

"He has all kinds of sayings about girl stuff." he replies. "This is his room."

We stop walking. I stare at the door, still scared of the greeting I'm about to get.

"You need me to knock for you?" Christopher offers in his chipper tone. I smile down at him.

"No kid, I got it." I laugh lightly as I ball my hand into a fist and knock on the wooden door.

"Ya gotta knock louder. Like this." he tells me. Before I can stop him, he's pounding on the door. "That'll wake him up if he's asleep."

I roll my eyes at him and shake my head slightly.

"Yeah, that'll do it. Why don't you go find your parents? I'll see you later."

"Awe alright." He sighs. "They're gonna start serving lunch any minute if you're hungry. See you there?"

"Maybe."

"Cool." he says and begins skipping down the hallway.

Once Christopher is gone, I knock on the door a third time.

"Shark?" I say through the door, "It's me, Scarlet."

I wait a few seconds before I see the door knob begin to turn. The door opens slowly and there he is.

He's dressed in a black T-shirt and a pair of jeans. He looks good in clean clothes. It doesn't look like he slept well, though. The circles around his eyes are dark, his face pale. He stares at me for a moment, probably deciding between sweeping me up in a hug and chopping my head off.

"Scarlet." His voice is a defeated whisper, "We were so worried." His eyes fill with tears.

Slowly I step forward, scared that he wouldn't want to hug me. He steps closer.

"I'm so sorry Shark. I don't know what I was thinking. I just was worried I was leading you into danger." I sob, wrapping my arms around his neck. I can feel his tears on my skin. "I'm sorry." I repeat. We stay that way for a long time, holding onto each other as if we were going to float away if we didn't.

I'm not afraid of him anymore, he's not mad. He was never going to be mad. He was scared. Of course he was scared.

Our already long moment was soon interrupted by the person I actually needed to be afraid of at the moment; Alec.

"Just when I thought we'd seen all your crazy. Was punching walls not enough for you? Picking fights with men twice your size? Now you just run off, in the middle of the night?!" I pull away from Shark and turn to face Alec, my eyes unable to meet his.

"Did you not think we'd follow you?" I look up to see the others coming up behind

"I thought you might." I reply sheepishly. If there was ever a time for the old Scarlet to pick a fight with Alec, now was it. But no, she was cowering in the back of my mind.

"If you ever pull something like that again." he growls.

"I just..." I want to explain. I want to tell them why I didn't want them to follow me.

"You just what?" Alec raises his voice. "You just wanted to scare us? You just wanted us to worry if you were dead? Is that what you wanted? Cause congrats! You pulled it off."

"No, I didn't want that." Here come the tears again. Don't cry, not now.

"Then what!" he shouts. My body begins to tremble.

"Do not yell at her like that." Shark steps in between the two of us. The two boys hold eachother's gaze.

I grab Sharks arm, take a deep breath and push him back behind me.

"I didn't want you to follow me." I finally admit, my eyes still not finding their way to Alec's.

"Why?" Alec finally lowers his voice. "What made you think we wouldn't?"

"Because," I lift my gaze, stepping away from Shark, "I need you guys to go home. I need you guys to stop following me. I'm bad luck, Alec." My eyes meet with Reese for a moment. She nods.

"Home? There is no home. Just an old, rickety building about to cave in on itself." Alec steps closer, his voice is beginning to shake. "What's happening to you Scarlet? What is it about this place that has you acting so weird?"

"I can't tell you." I mumble. He's standing over me now. Anger radiates off of him.

"Of course you can't." He snorts. "You never can anymore, can you? Always gotta be hiding something. Always gotta be the center of the drama. Right?"

"No Alec. That's not it." I kick the floor nervously.

"Then tell me. Tell me why this is so important. Tell me why we should pack up and leave you here."

"I can't." I sigh. "I tried." I say to Reese, tears now streaming down my face. Ally also turns to look at Reese. I squeeze in between Alec and Kevin, leaving the group standing there, feeling whatever it was we were all feeling in that moment.

How exactly am I supposed to tell them I don't want them here because I don't want to blow them up?

I lock myself in my room after that, tears still pouring out of my eyes. My hands find their way to my book bag. I unzip it and pull the device out, it's heavy. I toy with it gently and think.

This is what I came here for, I came here for revenge, for Kat, I came to finish what Evan started. But I wasn't planning on there being children here. I wasn't planning on there being normal people here. I pictured rich government officials and military leaders hiding out down here.

I imagined there being a big obvious red button, making it clear that they did this. But it's just people, just people surviving, just like me.

I pull out the plans I had written down and read them over. It seemed like the right thing then, but now it seems like insanity.

How did I become like this? Like Evan? So bent on revenge and destruction that I'm debating whether or not I should kill a bunch of children. I shove it back in my bag and slide it under my bed.

I can't blow this place up, can I?

* * *

It wasn't until Christopher came and got me for dinner that I left my room and I cried most of the time I was in there.

"Missed you at lunch, it was burgers today. They cook 'em real good too." he says immediately after I answered the door

"I'll have to try it next time." I force a smile. I imagine my eyes are still puffy from crying. He doesn't say anything. Although he seems like the type of kid that would.

"Well, it's pasta for dinner. It's not my favorite, but it's alright." He smiles. "How'd it go with your boyfriend?"

"It was fine." I say.

"He doesn't talk much, does he?" he says, "I went to get him for dinner and he just stared at me and then closed the door. "

"He'll get there eventually, he doesn't handle new places well." I reply.

"Ah well, guess it's his choice to starve."

"He'll be fine." I say more to myself than to Christopher.

"Well anyway, I suggest you get the white sauce instead of the red. I like tomato sauce, but the cooks here tend to spice it real weird for pasta night." His face is one of disgust.

I chuckle.

"So Scarlet, if you still want to meet Dr. Fowler tonight after dinner, I'm sure he'd love to meet you. And your friends, of course." Laura offers as we're all sitting around the table eating. I look around at the others, waiting for one of them to answer. Alec and I make eye contact for a short, uncomfortable moment.

"Um, yeah Laura, we'd love to meet him." I force a smile.

"Speak for yourself." I hear Reese grunt under her breath, but loud enough that both Alec and I hear her. She's glaring at me, but I don't look at her. I want to say something, but I wouldn't even know what to say.

"Maybe you two need to work this out in the hallway?" Alec suggests, his eyes shifting between the two of us. I can sense Laura's growing discomfort.

"I don't have anything to work out with her." I reply. "Or with you for that matter. No need to be dramatic."

"You obviously do." Alec's voice raises slightly, not enough to be a yell, but enough to get attention from the other people around us.

"Maybe you're the one with a problem." I mumble.

He glares at me for a long moment. I hope he'll forget about it and return to eating.

He doesn't.

"Okay, fine. Let's go." he finally says.

I roll my eyes, standing up and walking out without even checking to see if he's coming.

"What's your problem Alec?" I almost shout once we're both in the hall. "This place is quiet. These people are trying to enjoy a nice dinner. Why do you have to start crap in there like that?" My cheeks grow warm with embarrassment.

"I didn't start anything. You and Reese did." he argues.

"You're the one causing a scene in there."

"Fine, you really wanna know? You're my problem Scarlet.

You've been a problem ever since I met you. Going around punching walls, ordering us all around, pissing off Evan, need I go on?" He waits a second for me to reply. "You're impulsive and emotional. You've been running off doing who knows what for hours to days at a time. You were holding on to that backpack like it was your baby, and then you ran off, in the middle of the night leaving us to wonder where you went. How'd you even know where this thing was?" he yells.

"You're one to talk about disappearing for long periods of time Alec. Are you the only one entitled to mental breakdowns? You're the only one allowed to sneak off and drink a little and not come back for days? I'm not allowed to have space. Is that it?"

There she is, the girl who wasn't afraid to stand up to Alec.

"No." He's frustrated, but it doesn't last. His anger takes back its place in no time. "I would never have disappeared in the middle of the night to find the bunker on my own."

"I had to, Alec." I argue. Now would be a good time to think of a reason why.

"You had to?" He starts to laugh. "You had to?! That's what you keep saying, but you won't say why. You scared us to death! What if you were lost or..." He's breathing hard now. I'd swear if it wasn't Alec I'd think he was about to cry.

"Or dead?" I finish for him, my voice softening. "I'm sorry Alec, I didn't mean to scare you. I wasn't thinking straight."

"You never are." he replies. "You react based on your emotions. You never think before you do this kind of thing."

"I know. I'm sorry. I don't know what I'm doing Alec." I look down at my hands. "I've hit a dead end, I'm tired and I don't know where to go next. I thought this was my answer, I thought this was my out. I thought if I found this bunker I could do what I needed to do and I would feel like I have control again." I ramble.

"What is it you needed to do?" he asks. His hand is on my shoulder now.

"I just..." I raise now watery eyes to look at him. "I can't tell you." I sigh.

"Why?" He tries to control his tone. "It can't be that bad."

"I just can't tell you Alec." I repeat. "It doesn't matter now anyway."

"Alright." Alec sighs. "You don't have to explain yourself. But you have to stop acting stupid. I'm tired of it. Shark and I can't keep chasing after you like this." He stops himself and embraces me in a hug. I feel somehow both relieved and terrified.

"Scarlet, my mom wants to know if you want to meet Uncle Nathan now." Christopher says peeking his head into the hall.

"Uh, yeah." I sniff, wiping under my eyes before I look at him. "I'm coming." Christopher attempts to push the door open further. Alec grabs it to help him. I expect the kid to refuse the help, and he opens his mouth as if he was going to but then he just shrugs and lets go of the door completely.

I remember this feeling from the day I lost it at Alec's. The feeling that everyone was staring at you, that everyone's waiting for you to snap again. I'm waiting for me to snap again.

I direct my attention to the man talking to Laura. He's tall and slender. He doesn't look old, but he doesn't look young either. He's an attractive and charming looking man.

"Nathan this is Scarlet and Alec." Laura gestures to us. Her eyes scan me up and down, it's not as warm of a feeling as I'm used to getting from her.

146

"Ah, yes. Christopher told me a lot about you this afternoon." Doctor Fowler grins. "It's very nice to meet you."

"It's nice to meet you too." I reply, offering him my hand. He takes it and shakes it gently.

"My sister was telling me you have a lot of questions about our bunker."

"I did, but I feel like Laura answered them very well last night." I reply, I see Alec raise an eyebrow out of the corner of my eye.

"I'm glad my sister could be so informative." he says, still smiling, "If you want to know anything else let me know. I'm happy to explain anything you want to know." He seems kind, like the others, but I just have this feeling. Something's not right. I'm probably just being paranoid.

"Thank you, sir. I will." I reply.

"Of course."

At this point the tension in the room is strong. The two of us stand there, searching each other's eyes, looking for some reason to hate the other.

Although, I don't feel like I really need much of a reason. I already hate him, I already blame him.

"Well, if you all will excuse us, we have to find Richard and get to our meeting." Doctor Fowler breaks the silence. "It was lovely to meet you, Scarlet." His grin is unsettling now.

"You too Doctor." I reply. I watch as he walks out of the room. Laura and Christopher behind him.

I sit down at the table and lean into the others. They lean in as well.

"There was something off about that guy right?" I ask them.

Reese rolls her eyes slightly, "There's something off about

this whole place."

"Maybe he wouldn't have seemed so hostile, if you weren't asking so many questions." Alec replies.

"Maybe he wouldn't be so worried about me asking questions, if he had nothing to hide."

"Oh come on guys." Ally says. "Give it a chance. I like it here."

"Just, watch your backs guys." I sigh. "We don't know what they're up to."

"You're the one who insisted we come here in the first place." Reese glares at me. "I told you we shouldn't have."

"I didn't lead you here." I snap. "He did." I point at Alec.

Reese crosses her arms over her chest, her eyes shifting between Alec and I. Alec stands from the table and walks calmly out of the cafeteria.

"Reese." Ty rests his hand on her shoulder. "Let's take a walk." he suggests. The two of them stand up, leaving me with Ally and Kevin.

We sit in silence. Ally obviously upset by the idea of having to leave already.

"We know you're just trying to keep us safe. I trust you." Kevin says calmly. He leads Ally out of the room and I'm alone.

I laugh at myself for a moment. No, it's not funny. Just pathetic.

13

Shark

Morning came slow. I dressed myself in a dark shirt and jeans. I met with Nathan in his private dining hall. He told me to stay in character, to stay a part of the group. Until he can be sure that the group isn't going to try something. I have to convince Scarlet not to use the bomb, somehow. He's already suspicious. If he finds that, she's dead.

I return to my room after breakfast and sit in there, daydreaming. I hadn't really realized how much time had passed until a knock on my door draws me out of my thoughts. I realize I look exhausted as I catch a look of my face in the mirror by the bed. My eyes are red, dark circles surrounding them. Another knock. Slowly I cross the floor, hesitant to answer.

"Shark?" I hear her say through the door. "It's me Scarlet."

My heart leaps a little. I'm relieved to hear her voice. Relieved that she's okay. I open the door slowly. There she is. Her hair is down, framing her face. I stare at her. Do I yell at her? Embrace her? She looks at me, awaiting a reaction.

"Scarlet." I whisper breathlessly. After talking to Nathan

yesterday, I wasn't sure if I would see her again. I had almost given up on keeping her safe. "We were so worried." My eyes begin to water. I hate to cry in front of her. Hate for her to see me weak and defeated, but I can't help it. She slowly steps towards me. I step closer to her.

"I'm so sorry Shark. I don't know what I was thinking. I just was worried I was leading you into danger." She sobs. Her arms now wrapped around my neck. "I'm sorry." I hear her repeat. I hold her while the two of us cry. It's so good to hold her again. Unfortunately, our moment is cut short by someone who's not as happy to see her.

The fight with Alec is short lived but obviously took its toll on Scarlet. I stand helpless, as I watch her sulk away down the hall. The others turn and leave, as if they didn't see the interaction I'd just witnessed. As if they didn't care at all about how Alec had made her feel. If only they understood.

I conceal myself in my room for the next few hours. I find myself thinking about Scarlet, I know the bomb is taking a toll on her. I also know she'll never be safe hiding it here. I have to get it from her somehow.

Around six, Christopher comes knocking on my door.

"Hey Chris, what's up?" I greet him. He's smiling warmly at me.

"Dinner." he says. "Mom says you can starve if ya wanna, but she prefers you alive."

"Dinner? Oh yeah that sounds good." I smile. I hadn't realized I was hungry until he mentioned food.

"Come on, you can see what room your girlfriend's in when we pick her up."

"We're picking her up?" I think on this for a moment. Then the idea hits me. If I can get into her room while she's at dinner, I can get the bomb. I'll get it out of here, and she'll be safe. They all will be.

"Shark?" Chris draws me out of my thoughts by waving his hand in my face.

"You know what? I'm not hungry." I tell him. "But could you...could you show me her room? I need to get something out of her backpack."

"Is this some kind of secret spy thing?" A grin spreads across his face. I think for a moment.

"Sure." I chuckle.

"So cool! What do ya want me to tell her?"

"Anything. You just have to get her out of the room and to dinner. Then I'll sneak in and get what I need."

"Alright let's go!" He begins to eagerly skip down the hall. I follow him, nearly having to jog to keep up.

"Okay, stay here." he whispers to me. "I'll go get her." I watch as he walks up to her door and knocks. My eyes are fixed on them. She looks like she's been crying, my heart sinks. I know that this will take some weight off of her. But I wish I could do so much more. I watch as Christopher begins leading her towards the cafeteria. I walk towards her room. Almost there, a couple of seconds and this will all be over.

"Hey, Finn!" RIchards voice startles me. I freeze for a moment, my eyes wide. He places his hand on my shoulder. "Or...Shark, I'm sorry. It's taking me some time to get used to that alias. Anyway, how are you holding up?"

"I'm alright Richard." I respond. What does he want? He's rarely in the mood for smalltalk.

"Good, good." He pauses to think. "Would you mind if we talked in your room?" he asks.

I can't tell him no. I look at her door and frown. Hopefully, this doesn't take long and I can get in and out of there. I nod and begin to lead him down the hall towards my room.

"What is this about Richard?" I ask as I turn the doorknob. He shakes his head, his expression serious. We shuffle in quickly, closing the door quietly behind us. "Richard?" I ask again once we're inside.

"It's Nathan," he begins, "I'm afraid he's decided to proceed with the second half of phase two."

"Phase two? With what research? Evan burnt it all months ago."

"Maybe so, but Nathan is convinced that your girlfriend may know something to help."

"She doesn't." I lie. "They were enemies, he didn't share any information with her."

"Enemies?" He raises an eyebrow. "That's not what your reports say."

No, it's not. Back then I was more concerned with my mission than I was her safety. I reported back that Evan seemed to be recruiting Scarlet for something. I never reported the fight or what happened after. As far as they know, Evan was alive and plotting with Scarlet up until earlier this week.

"Finn, Nathan didn't send me. Laura did. She's worried that you and your friends may be in danger."

I meet his gaze. Do I tell him? I've always been able to trust Laura.

"Nathan is paranoid that your friends are going to try something. After Carrie's death, he hasn't been very trusting of anybody. Whether your girlfriend has Evan's research or not, you are all still in danger."

"I know." I sigh.

"If you tell me what's going on, Laura and I may be able to help you. To keep you informed at least."

"Evan had a plan to come back and destroy the bunker, he had his sights set on revenge. Shortly after meeting Scarlet, he began to recruit her. She turned him down, she wasn't going to help him. He got so mad Richard." I find myself saying. It wasn't planned. I didn't mean to, but it came out anyway. "He beat her. He nearly killed her." My voice grows shaky as the anger rises in my chest. I picture her face that day, bloodied and bruised. "So I killed him."

"It's okay, keep going." Richard says. His voice is oddly comforting. He's not searching my words for information anymore. He sits and listens as I unload the trauma from the last few months.

"I killed him and I thought she was over it. We all knew she was angry about the attacks. They all were. We hurt so many people. She was losing control, everyone was. But Scarlet was spiralling hard. The burden of it really got to her and she began to plot again. She used Evan's plans and maps. She would disappear for hours, sometimes days. She became obsessed."

"So she did have Evan's research?"

I look Richard in the eyes as a think through what I say next, "No. She *has* his bomb." I clarify. The air grows still for a moment. Did I put her in more or less danger by telling him that?

"She has it here?"

I nod, "I didn't think she'd go this far Richard. She's not like Evan, she's not ruthless and vengeful. But she has it here, I think it's in her room."

"That would be enough to complete the research needed." Richard sighs. He checks his watch and then returns his gaze to me. "If he finds out about this, he'll kill all of them. This would give him the power to kill millions more."

"I know. I was planning to sneak into her room and get it out of here. While she was away at dinner."

"Better hurry then, you have 20 minutes before dinner is over." He walks towards the door.

"Hold on to that bomb once you find it. We may have another use for it. We'll talk more soon." He leaves the room. I wait a moment before going back to her room. I'll have to be fast, she could come back at any minute.

"Shark?" I hear her voice as I begin to turn the doorknob, "What are you doing?"

"Oh, hey Scarlet. I..." I turn to look at her, my cheeks grow warm. What do I do now? Richard's expecting me to get the bomb.

"Are you alright? Christopher said you didn't feel like coming to dinner." She reaches for my hand.

"I'm fine." I sigh. Although I'm not, at all. I feel defeated. If Nathan thinks she knows something, it's only a matter of time before he does something about it. I'm so scared that I'll lose her to him. All because of that stupid bomb.

"What are you doing outside my room?" she asks suspiciously.

"I was just looking for you." I answer. My face is tense. I hope she buys it, she has to. If she thinks that I don't trust her, I'll never get that bomb. I'll never be able to keep her safe.

"Well, here I am." She shrugs, smiling her sad smile. As I look at her, I feel myself softening.

"Yeah, here you are." I find myself smiling slightly.

"You sure you're okay? You don't look good."

I stare at her for a long moment. Her eyes so sad. I wish I could take all of this away from her. All the memories of the past few months. All her hurt.

I squeeze her hand, "It's not important now." I reply. As much as I know I have to get that bomb out of here. To protect her. I just want to be with her. To talk to her now. To not have to worry about all of this craziness.

"Do you want to come in and talk?"

I nod. I watch her turn the handle and follow her into the room. All of these rooms are identical except for whatever wall decorations are hanging on the wall. I scan the room quickly for her bag, spotting it poking out just from under her bed. I walk over to the bed and sit on the edge of it.

I find myself ranting to her about how worried I am for her. She promises she won't do something stupid. I'm not sure if I believe her. I know the bunker wasn't what she was expecting. I'm sure she's second guessing herself. But this is Scarlet, she'll do something impulsive eventually. I try to subtly warn her about the dangers of having a bomb under her bed. Hiding one in the bunker.

I choose to believe that for now, she won't do anything. I kiss her gently.

"I'm sorry I scared you." she apologizes as she pulls away. I know she's sorry. She never means to hurt us when she does these things.

"I love you." I tell her.

"I love you too."

"I really do." I whisper.

Maybe I should be the one feeling guilty here? She doesn't

even know who I am, not really. She loves Shark, caring, loving, protective Shark. But that's not who I am. I'm Finn. A follower, a coward. Always caught on the wrong side of things. She wouldn't love Finn, he's not a good guy. I hope she never has to meet him. I hope that somehow this ends before she gets the chance. I sigh, laying down. I stare thoughtfully at the ceiling. She rests her head on my chest. I find myself wishing this was how things could be forever. I wish things could be this simple all of the time. Just the two of us, together. I drift to sleep, holding on to her.

14

Scarlet

I lay on the bed, Sharks deeps breaths tell me that he's fallen asleep. I smile at the thought of my head on his chest. I listen to his steady heartbeat as if it's a lullaby, the best lullaby I've ever heard. In the stillness of the night, I feel my mind begin to wander towards suspicion. I wonder what brought Shark to my room this evening. Was it really just to talk? Did he only come to tell me he loves me? A large part of me hopes so, what a dream that would be to have him find me just to tell me that. But, deep in my heart, I feel like that wasn't the reason.

I come to the paranoid conclusion that he suspects something. He knows that I'm plotting and he came to find out why. He may have come to talk me out of it. But then why didn't he? Why attempt to break in my room to talk me out of a scheme and not do it? I twist my head awkwardly to look at him, just for a moment. I supposed he could have just come to be with me. Perhaps he did just want to talk.

I push the worried thoughts from my mind and focus my senses on the rise and fall of his chest. I match my breathing to his, fully in sync with his breaths.

"Goodnight." I whisper to him, though I know he's in too deep a slumber to hear me. I close my eyes and allow myself to fall asleep there, protected in his arms. Feeling truly safe for the first time since the attacks.

* * *

Morning comes fast. I wake to the sound of someone banging on the door. I groan, reluctantly getting myself out of bed. Shark sits up slightly, he looks a little disoriented.

"It's probably just Christopher getting us up for breakfast." I tell him, looking at the clock hanging on the wall next to the door. I open the door, expecting to see the young, blonde boy standing outside but it's not him.

"Ally!" I greet her, surprised. She peeks her head into my room, seeing Shark on the bed.

"Morning Scarlet. Shark." She winks at Shark. She seems more hyper than she has been in a long time, much like the day I met her and Kat.

"Morning Ally." Shark replies uncomfortably.

"Scarlet, I need your help." She pushes past me into my room and sits down on the bed. I shrug at Shark.

"Okay?" I close the door.

"So, there's this boy." She starts. I sit close beside her on the bed. "I ran into him last night...like literally. And just, Scarlet his smile and his eyes were so green and Scarlet, he's my age and you gotta help me!" She grabs my hand and squeezes it.

"I'm gonna go back to my room and get a shower." Shark says, rolling out of bed. I hear him say it, but I'm too caught up in what Ally is saying to remember to respond. He slips quietly out of the room, leaving us alone.

"Tell me more." I giggle. It's fun to be able to talk about a boy like I'm in high school and everything's back to the way it was.

Ally goes on telling me all about him, explaining every detail she noticed. It's cute seeing her so excited.

"What's his name?" I ask once she's done.

"Oh... uh, I didn't think to ask." She blushes.

"Come on." I look at the clock and pull her up off of the bed. "Breakfast should be going on now. I bet he'll be there. You can ask him then."

"Uh." She scoots slowly behind me. "Ask him?"

"Yeah, for his name." I pause, "Come on."

"Fine, But I'm only coming because I'm hungry." She agrees, allowing me to continue pulling her in the direction of the cafeteria.

Ally stops abruptly before walking through the door to the cafeteria.

"What?" I ask her, slightly annoyed, completely starving.

"He's in there." she whispers. I look around the room as if I know what the boy looks like.

"Where?" I ask her after realizing that there are two teens that look the way she described.

"Right there," She points subtly, "At the third table."

"Okay, well go in!" I pull the door open, practically pushing her through. "I'm hungry."

Awkwardly, she grabs a plate, trying to look like she isn't staring at him. He notices her standing in line and keeps stealing a look in our direction every couple of seconds, she doesn't catch him.

After serving our breakfast, I lead her to the second table and sit down right in front of him, facing away.

"What are you doing." She mouths to me as she sits down across the table. I just shrug and begin shoveling food into my mouth. She looks up at him, makes eye contact and smiles nervously at him. Quickly she looks back down at her plate. Her face flushes bright red.

Not too long after the others come and sit with us. Reese sits beside Ally, Shark beside me.

"What're we talkin' about?" Kevin asks, instantly sensing that something was up.

"Probably the boy Ally likes." Shark says loudly. I elbow him, spilling the food on his fork in his lap.

Ally rests her forehead on the palm of her hand and laughs nervously.

"Oh? Who's that Ally?" Kevin teases. At this point all of us are trying not to laugh at poor Ally's reaction to us picking on her.

"Okay, don't look." I begin. Ally's glaring at me. "But the guy directly behind me, facing Ally." I tell them as quietly as I can. Reese looks up for a moment.

"Oh he is cute." She leans in towards Ally.

"Oh, you like Sam?" Christopher says as he sits on the other side of me. I hadn't even seen him come in.

"Hey Sam!" The kid shouts to the boy behind me.

"Morning Chris!" Sam replies.

"Come over here and meet the newbies." he calls back, waving him over.

"Oh no." Ally groans. At this point Kevin is laughing so uncontrollably he's trying not to spit his water all over the table.

Sam walks over and stands at the end of the table. Ally was right about his smile, it is precious. He's pretty well in shape, a little on the short side but he's cute.

Christopher introduces us all, emphasizing Ally. Sam greets us, his eyes not leaving Ally. Not that she could see him staring at her as she was pretending to have a conversation with Reese.

"Sam's the coolest." Christopher says, grinning wide. "He lets me hang out with him when my parents are doing... whatever it is that my parents do." The pride Christopher takes from just knowing Sam is adorable.

"Well, it's nice to meet you Sam." I say to him. "Do you want to sit with us?"

At that Ally has stopped pretending to have a conversation and is frozen, her eyes wide.

"Sure." Sam shrugs.

"You can sit here." Kevin says, scooting over to make room for him next to Ally. Now Shark and I are laughing. I grab his hand and squeeze it, he squeezes back.

"Oh, um." Sam stares at the empty seat for a long moment. "Okay." He blushes a little as he takes his seat next to Ally, who is desperately trying to non-verbally get Reese to scoot over so she can scoot away from him. Reese doesn't budge.

"So, how are you guys liking it here?" Sam asks us all.

"I mean I'm liking it a lot so far. It's nice having electricity and good food." Kevin replies. "What about you Ally? You like it here?" Kevin directs the attention to Ally. I hear her gulp. Her wide eyes shift towards Sam.

"Oh um, it's nice." she replies. Her knee begins to bounce nervously.

"I'm glad you like it." Sam smiles again, staring at Ally.

"How long have you been here Sam?" I ask him. Hoping to

relieve Ally a bit by taking his attention off of her for a moment.

"Oh, since maybe three days before the bombs hit New Mexico." he says.

"You here with your family?" I ask.

"Just my mom and my little sister," I try to not be jealous that his family is still alive. "What about you guys?" he asks.

"No, this is it. Our families didn't make it." I tell him, my heart sinks a little.

"Oh. I'm sorry." He frowns. There's awkward silence for a moment after.

"Hey Sam, you should show Ally around." Christopher suggests. Sam thinks for a moment, waiting for Ally to say something. She doesn't. She's probably too nervous to think about it.

"Would you like a tour?" he asks her. She finally looks at him for the first time.

"Uh...yeah, okay." She accepts reluctantly.

"Awesome." He grins. "Let's go." He stands up, she follows suit.

"Cool." She giggles uncomfortably.

"Have fun you two." Kevin says, trying to sound as much like a mom as he could. We all watch as Sam leads Ally out of the cafeteria, holding the door for her and asking her questions.

"Ah, young love." Kevin chuckles. "Isn't that refreshing?"

We all turn to look at Christopher.

"What?" He shrugs. "It looked like they needed a little help."

Our table erupts in a fit of laughter. My stomach aches, but I can't stop laughing, and I don't want to.

* * *

"So...Ally's got a boyfriend now." Alec chuckles lightly. The two of us are sitting in the cafeteria, while the others are exploring the bunker.

"I guess so." I smile. "We probably scared the poor kid pretty bad though."

"No, Kevin scared him." He corrects me.

"Well, yeah. Poor Ally didn't look very happy."

"No, but I'm sure that's changed by now."

"So, maybe you were right." I say. "Maybe this place isn't so bad. I haven't seen Ally that happy in a long time." Swallowing my pride and admitting that isn't quite as painful as I thought.

"Neither have I." He frowns thoughtfully for a moment. "I know you wanted to find something wrong with this place Scarlet, and I understand. But I don't think you'll find it here. I think this place is what it looks like."

"Maybe you're right." I agree doubtfully. "So, you think we should stay?"

"I don't see a better option."

"Well, then I guess this is home, at least for now."

Part of me does feel defeated, but mostly I'm hopeful. We're not alone anymore, we don't have to fend for ourselves anymore.

"Come on, let's go explore with the others." Alec stands up. "I hear there's a gym."

"Yeah. It's a pretty nice gym." I stand with him. "Let's go."

I find myself leading him on a tour of the bunker, remembering everything Christopher told me to the best of my ability.

"And this is the library." I tell Alec as I lead him into the last room.

He gasps, taking in the giant room filled to the ceiling with books.

"This is huge!" he exclaims.

"I know." I laugh a little. "It's pretty big. I wonder when they had the time to build this."

"Scarlet." He shoots me a look.

"I know, I'm sorry." I raise my hands slightly. "It's just a little suspicious."

On the other end of the room, I see Doctor Fowler talking to Richard. They're sitting at one of the ten large, square, oak tables in the back of the first floor of the library.

The doctor notices the two of us and waves. I wave back, but quickly walk over to the closest shelf and pretend to look through the titles.

"What'd you do that for?" Alec asks me, puzzled.

"I don't know." I shrug, still looking at the books. "He just makes me uncomfortable."

"We should go say hi." he suggests. I stop and glare at him. "Why?"

"I don't know, cause it'd be polite."

"Since when are we worried about being polite?"

"Since he's the guy who's in-charge and it'd be good if he liked us. Not to mention you managed to tick him off already after you've only been here two days."

"You make a good point." I roll my eyes.

I begin walking slowly towards the two men.

"Good afternoon Doctor Fowler." I greet him. "Richard."

Richard smiles warmly at me.

"Good afternoon Scarlet." Doctor Fowler replies dryly. "How've you been enjoying your time here?"

"I think it's growing on me."

"Well, I'm happy to hear it." he replies. Something about his tone makes me uneasy.

"I'm in love with this library."

I can almost hear Alec's thoughts telling me not to ask.

"How long did it take to build it? It must have taken ages."

"Well," The doctor's eyes narrow, "We had a rather large crew so it didn't take all that long actually."

"And everyone from that same crew is still here?"

"Quite a few, some of them went to California or Nevada to help with those shelters."

"Wow! Other shelters?"

"Yes, there are many other shelters. Four just in California."

"I guess you and your crew were very well prepared." I don't know what I'm trying to accuse him of.

"Miss Scarlet, these bunkers were built long before any threats or theories of threats had ever reached the US. I'm afraid whatever idea you have of what is going on here is not what's going on." Doctor Fowler steps towards me in a threatening manner.

"Well, that's some interesting stuff. Thank you for your time Doctor." I chicken out of asking anything more.

"Yes, well. If you would like to know anything more, there are a number of books about the bunkers in this library." he replies. "I'll just assume you don't need my help finding those. Do you?" His tone is condescending now.

"No sir, I think I'll do just fine finding what I need." Even I'm not sure if that was meant to be a threat or not.

"Good." he replies. "Well, I'll leave you to peruse the literature. Richard and I have some work to get done this afternoon." He brushes my shoulder as he walks past us.

"Really?" Alec finally speaks after they've left the room.

"I know." I sigh. "I just couldn't help it."

"You always did have a thing for testing authority."

"I do, but also that man just doesn't like me."

"Well, maybe because you just implied that he had something to do with the attacks."

"I know, I know." I frown, rubbing the back of my neck. "But you have to admit he was being oddly defensive."

"Not everyone who's being defensive is guilty."

"I know." I sigh. "This is your fault, you know."

"No. It's not."

"Come on Scarlet let's go say hi. It's the polite thing to do. He'll like us." I do my best impression of Alec.

"Are you mocking me right now?" He raises an eyebrow. I smirk slightly.

"I'm just saying he might not hate me if I hadn't been pushed to go say hello."

"It's not my fault you have Shark's social skills." He rolls his eyes.

"Other than the doctor hating me, what do you think? You think this could be home?" I change the subject.

"Don't know." He shrugs. "I think it's safe. We're fed, clean and well rested. Ally's met a boy, and the people seem nice."

"That a yes?" I raise my eyebrows. I almost hope he'll say no.

"Why don't we gather the others for a meeting and get their opinions?" he suggests. I agree.

The two of us split up in search of the other five.

* * *

It doesn't take us very long to round the others up and soon we're all sitting around my room.

"Alright guys, we made it. We're in the bunker." I start.

"Really? I hadn't noticed." Reese mumbles.

I ignore her.

"So, what do you guys think?" I ask.

"It doesn't seem too bad." Ally replies.

"Well of course you don't think so." Kevin teases, pushing her playfully.

"Quit it." She laughs, her cheeks turning pink.

"I think it's better than where we were before." Alec says.

"I agree." I nod. "So, we can stay or we can go back. But we'll make this decision together."

"I think we should go back." Reese says. I watch Ty pinch his lips together. "I know this place is great. It has the luxuries that we had before the attacks. But Doctor Fowler is hiding things. Things that I don't think we want to know."

"Like what Reese?" Ally asks, genuinely curious.

Reese leans into Ty.

"It's okay Reese. I got it." Ty says to her, grabbing her hand. "When we were here before, Reese and Kat overheard Nathan and Carrie. Carrie was Nathan's wife. They were talking about the bombings. Nathan saw Kat and threatened her." Kevin and Ty exchange a look.

"Later, Kat confronted Carrie about it. She said she was just trying to get Carrie to tell her what the conversation was about. Kat couldn't get it out of her. It must have been a pretty big deal though because Carrie pulled a gun on Kat." Kevin says. Taking over for Ty. "Ty, Reese and I heard the gunshots from our rooms and came out into the hall to see Kat standing over Carrie. There was blood covering the floor."

"We all ran." Reese says. "We just ran."

"Reese are you in danger if you're here?" I ask her, now realizing why she didn't want to come.

"I don't know." She shrugs. "Nobody's said anything. I'm not even sure they know we were a part of it at all. But Doctor Fowler doesn't seem like the kind to forget."

"Well, that changes things." Alec sighs.

"Does it?" I ask. "It doesn't have to. For once, we are fed, hydrated, clean, and safe like you said earlier. We don't actually know what that conversation was about. We can play dumb, pretend we don't know anything at all." I suggest.

"Play dumb?" Reese glares at me.

"Reese, if you weren't safe here, they would've done something when you first showed up. So we'll just pretend you guys didn't tell us all of that and we'll live here as normally as we can, for as long as we can."

"It's not safe here." Reese argues. "Fowler is smart, and probably pretty pissed that Kat shot his wife. I'm sure that if he hasn't figured out who we are yet, he will, and it won't be safe for any of us."

"Let's just stay." I plead, ignoring her. "We deserve to be happy and safe and we can't do that out there."

"Reese." Ty says. "She's right. If they thought we were part of it, they would've killed us. They don't know who we are. We're safe here."

"Fine." She finally agrees. "We'll stay, but if this goes wrong, it's not on me."

"Is everyone cool with that?" Alec asks.

They all agree with a hint of reluctance.

"Then let's go get some dinner." I hold the door as the group files out of my room.

"You sure this is right?" Alec asks me once the others far enough down the hall. "You're the one who didn't trust any of this up front. Now you have a reason"

"No, but they deserve to be happy Alec. We all do." I reply. "And I don't know how else to do that for them."

"Why are you so convinced that this place is so good all of the sudden?" he asks me. I watch the others disappear around the corner. "Are you convinced?"

"No, I'm not convinced, something still seems off. But I need to keep believing that these people are good."

"Because?"

"Because that crazy chick you keep accusing me of being. She's still here." I point to my head. "And if I stop believing they're good, what would happen next would just..." I stop, feeling my eyes begin to water. For the first time since I gave into Evan's crazy plan, I feel ashamed. I feel embarrassed that I let myself get this far. I feel the urge to tell him, but I can't.

"Just what?"

"You would hate me..." I admit, a sob escapes from my mouth. "If I told you what I wanted so badly to do. What I still feel like I need to do."

"Why." He wraps me in a hug. "Why would I hate you?" And here it is.

If I had words to speak, they were held back by sob after sob. Everything in me trembles as tears run down my face.

"Scarlet, whatever's going on. Whatever made you run away, whatever made you disappear for days back at the house. It won't make me hate you. You can tell me." It's weird being comforted by Alec. Sure, I've seen his soft side. I knew it existed. But the two of us have always butted heads, we've been at each other's throats since the day we met. Yet here he is, being perfectly human, comforting me.

Finally, after a long cry and a long silence from Alec, I catch my breath, wipe my tears and look him in the eye.

Should I tell him? If I tell him will it change how he sees me?

"I'm worried I'm crazy." I tell him. Suddenly my body relaxes and I feel calm. But it doesn't seem like a good calm. It's not the calm that comes after something, not relief. More like waiting for something big, something dramatic to happen. "I'm paranoid, all the time."

"If this is about what I said when I got here, I didn't mean—" He begins to apologize.

"No, no. I mean, yes, but only because it was true Alec. It's like ever since the bombs I've started losing piece after piece of myself and I thought I was doing a good thing." I take a breath.

"But I just." I choke back another sob. *No Scarlet, you've cried enough.* "I wanted to believe that there was somebody out there, somebody I could get to who's responsible. Somebody that I could punish, some way I could gain control of this craziness and get revenge."

"Revenge? On who?"

My chest grows tight as I convince my mind and my mouth to allow me to be honest.

"I guess Evan got in my head. All his talk about the bunkers, about how suspicious it was that they suddenly started popping up before the attacks. Like they knew what was coming. And I kept thinking. The only way they would know it was coming was if they did it. I don't know how or why, but I just believed that. I needed to blame somebody." I take another breath. "I keep losing people over this and I'm so mad. And even if they didn't bomb the country, they still knew and they did nothing. Everyone died, Alec. Everyone. My parents, my friends, Kat...

even Evan died. Maybe he deserved it, maybe not." I look to see if he's still listening to me ramble on.

"He did deserve it." he grumbles.

"Maybe. But his theories; overpopulation, the government bombing the states. Maybe they put bunkers in place to harbor a set amount of people, maybe they bought their way in here. I don't know, it just made sense. After talking to Doctor Fowler in the library it seemed to make even more sense."

"Scarlet, Evan was insane. He was angry. He wanted to take it out on someone. His theories weren't true." Alec begins to whisper, making me aware that we're still in the hallway.

We shuffle back into my room before continuing.

"Evan was willing to murder all of these people on a theory."

I drop my gaze to the floor. I feel like I have to tell him. I bend down and grab my bag out from under my bed.

"He had it all planned out before he died. Maps, blueprints, and this." I unzip the bag. Alec looks at it, confused.

"What is that?" he asks. His voice says he knows, but he's hoping he's wrong.

"Evan's bomb."

"Why do you have it?" I can't tell if he's mad or not.

"He built it, but I've been planning this, fantasizing about it for weeks." I admit. "I don't know what's wrong with me Alec. It got in my head and I've been obsessed with the idea of it. But I'm not going through with it. After I met Laura and Richard. After I met Christopher I changed my mind." I try to redeem myself.

"The idea of detonating a bomb on innocent people?" He begins to pace back and forth. "You're right, that is insane. Evan made all of that stuff up Scarlet. He needed to blame somebody. Why would you even consider it? Bring a bomb here?"

"I guess I needed somebody to blame too. I wanted somebody to pay and after Kat, I wanted it so much more."

"I knew you were hiding something." he sighs. "A bomb Scarlet? If they find that, who knows what they'll do."

"They won't find it." I reply. "I'll find some way to get rid of it. I promise."

"I just...I can't right now."

I watch as he walks out of the room, letting the door slam behind him.

I sit on my bed, alone. The shame reveals itself to me again now that I'm sitting in silence. I don't cry this time, though. I just stare. I stare emotionlessly at Evan's bomb and I think. I wonder again how I became this, a person, so overrun with anger that she was willing to murder a bunch of people based on the theory of a madman.

* * *

I've been sitting in the same position throughout the whole night. I flip between feeling guilty and feeling empty. I feel almost like a robot now as I change into clean clothes. I pause and stare at myself in the mirror until I don't like what I look like anymore.

I open my door to see Christopher standing in front of it, his hand balled up like I caught him mid-knock.

"Hey kid." I force a smile. I wish I could genuinely feel happy to see him.

"Mornin'." he replies, chipper as always. "You missed dinner last night so I thought I'd come make sure you remembered when breakfast was."

"That's very sweet Chris." Even my voice sounds empty.

"Thanks!" He beams. "C'mon, I'm starving." He grabs my arm and pulls me down the hallway. I put a couple of pieces of fruit on my plate and join the others at their table.

Sam is sitting next to Ally who doesn't seem nervous around him anymore.

Shark grabs my hand under the table.

"That all you're gonna eat?" Christopher asks, setting his plate on the table piled with waffles down across from me.

I shrug, poking my fruit with a fork.

"You alright Scarlet?" Ty asks.

I look at him and he nods, like a look into my eyes was all he needed to know.

Alec grunts quietly. I can feel his eyes on me. I refuse to meet his gaze.

"I'm just not hungry is all." I shrug again. Hoping that the others will return to eating in peace.

Suddenly, Alec stands up, grabs his dish and leaves the table. My eyes follow him as he dumps his plate and storms out of the room. I shudder as the door slams shut.

I begin to stand up, but Shark holds me back, shaking his head.

"What's with him?" Kevin asks. Rolling his eyes slightly.

"Just Alec being Alec." Ally replies. I take a deep breath, closing my eyes, hoping that when I open them, I won't feel this guilt anymore. It doesn't work.

"Yup, Alec being Alec." I mumble. Clearing my place and leaving the room.

"Hey." Shark follows me out of the cafeteria.

I can't look at him. I begin to walk down the hallway, ignoring that he's following close behind.

"Scarlet stop!" he calls after me. I'm not even sure where I'm going. I just know I don't want to deal with this right now. "Scarlet, I know."

I freeze. Know what? What does he know? He catches up to me, grabbing my upper arm gently.

"I know about the bomb." he whispers. His warm breath lingers on my ear, the word "bomb" echoing in my head.

"Alec." I sigh. I wait for him to say something. Wait for him to tell me what Alec told him.

"He told me what happened yesterday." He confirms. "But I already knew."

"You did? How?" I ask.

"I can't explain that right now." He looks at the floor.

"I have—" I lower my voice, "I have a bomb lying under my bed right now." Saying it out loud is different. I can't catch my breath anymore. I grab my chest.

"Okay, okay. Come on." He grabs my hand, looking around to make sure nobody heard us. He leads me into his room, quietly closing the door behind us.

"Shark, I have a bomb under my bed." I continue to hyper-ventilate.

"Calm down. We'll fix this. It will be fine." He holds me, trying to calm me down. "I'll take care of the bomb."

"If you get caught sneaking a bomb out of my room, who knows what they'll do." I reply.

"I won't get caught." he argues. "Let me handle it. Scarlet, you can't say another word about any of this."

"I won't." I promise. "But this is my mess, let me handle it."

"Would you stop being so stubborn?" he shouts. "Let me handle it before you get yourself shot. These people aren't gonna mess around if they find out you have one of Evan's bombs."

"What do you mean one of Evan's bombs?" I look at him.

"I misspoke." He rolls his eyes. "Can you just let me handle this before you get caught and killed for this? Please."

I glare at him. Maybe he did misspeak, but I just can't help but feel like maybe he's hiding something too.

Why would he specify that it's Evan's? Does that mean something?

"I said no Shark. I meant no." I tell him firmly. I walk out of his room.

I walk away, down the hall. I can't get my mind off of it. There's something he isn't telling me. I can feel it.

15

Shark

"A bomb?" I raise my eyebrows, trying to act like I didn't already know about the bomb Scarlet's been carrying with her all this time. The two of us stand across from each other in my room discussing Alec's conversation with Scarlet from yesterday, just after we had all had a meeting about whether or not we should stay. I guess that Scarlet told Alec everything and as expected, Alec didn't take it very well.

"Yes Shark, a bomb." Alec repeats himself impatiently.

"How did we not know?"

Alec shrugs, "I don't know. She said she wasn't going to use it. I don't know Shark, I don't trust that she won't."

"Give her some credit Alec, she won't kill all of these innocent people."

"You don't know that! Scarlet's lost her mind. Can't you see that?"

"She isn't insane."

"How is this not insane? She wants to blow up this bunker because of something that Evan told her."

"She's just upset."

"Just upset?" Alec scoffs. "Wake up man! She's having some sort of weird mental breakdown. Because of that, she's going to get us and everyone in this place killed.."

I take a deep breath, raising my hand to rub the back of my neck. I know he's right. Why can't I admit that to him? I know how Scarlet can be, that when she's determined she loses control over herself. That's why I need to get the bomb from her. Before she snaps.

"Shark," he says, placing his hand gently on my shoulder, "she's gone. Sane Scarlet has left the building and I'm not sure she's ever coming back. We can try to stop her but you and I both know she won't listen. I say we pack up the crew and leave before she brings us down with her."

Anger swells in my stomach as I replay his words in my mind. I find myself grabbing him by the collar of his shirt and slamming his body hard against the wall. Heat rises to my cheeks as I breathe heavily through my clenched teeth. I don't remember thinking that I was going to do that, it just happened.

"We can't just leave her here! She's just going through a lot, she'll come back to her senses soon. She just watched somebody die Alec! And it broke her, it broke all of us. Leaving her would kill her."

Alec kicks me in the groin causing me to drop him and stumble backwards, before I can block him his fist connects with my jaw sending a shock of pain through my whole head. I stare at him in shock. He steps closer to me and I flinch, though he doesn't move to harm me.

"We're all going through a lot right now Shark. But only one of us is considering murdering innocent people. Only one of us has been acting erratically since the day she showed up. I can't watch out for her anymore. She's on her own."

"So you're fine with leaving her to die?" I raise my voice. "Doesn't she matter to you?"

"I tried Shark! We both tried. We were there for her. We watched out for her. I backed up every single one of her insane ideas back at the house. I have extended grace upon grace when she's given me nothing but disrespect and defiance. She's too far gone man. Give up. We can't save her anymore."

"Give up." I scoff, "Just give up. And lose her like we lost Kat? We can't let her destroy herself Alec and it's not fair of you to ask me to. I know that you're pissed that she didn't tell you about the bomb, but this is why. Look at how you're reacting." I pause for a breath, stepping towards him. "It's Scarlet. I can't watch her implode, not after everything we've been through together. We can't give up on her, not yet."

Alec's eyes meet with mine but quickly shift to the floor.

"If it were Ally, you would drag her out of this yourself. If she were the one falling apart and losing her grip, you would give yourself to save her. Hasn't Scarlet earned her place as our family? I've seen the way you watch out for her as if she were your own blood. So help me save her, please. We don't have much time left."

"In my family, we don't keep secrets." he spits. "I love her Shark, I do. But I can't help her anymore. You're on your own."

I silently plead with him one more time before I turn to leave for breakfast.

* * *

178

After breakfast and the conversation I had with Scarlet about the bomb, I find myself walking swiftly towards Richard and Laura's bunk, hoping that they'll be there. I run my hands nervously through my hair as I wait for somebody to answer the door.

"Finn," Laura scans me up and down before opening the door further to let me in. "What's wrong?"

"Is Richard here?" I ask. She nods, gesturing to the small dining area. Laura and Richard's room is bigger than most because they're Nathan's family. I follow her to the square table and sit down across from Richard. He looks at me and raises an eyebrow. Laura sits beside me, holding my hand while I catch my breath.

"I couldn't get it." I tell him. "I tried but I failed. I slipped up Richard." I can't tell if he's judging me for my weakness, but if he was, I wouldn't blame him. I was trained for this. I've been a soldier since I was fourteen. And then this girl comes in and wrecks everything and I can't pull off a simple mission anymore. Who am I? "And now Alec knows and he wants to leave her here without any protection from Nathan. What do I do? How do I fix this?"

"Take a deep breath sweetheart, calm down." Laura squeezes my hand and looks to Richard.

"I'm losing her Laura, and I don't know how to help her. I could see that she knew I was lying to her this morning."

"She's going through a lot, and so are you." She comforts me. Richard studies me from across the table. "We'll help you figure this out."

"How did you slip up?" Richard finally asks.

"I told her I know she has Evan's bomb. I specifically said 'Evan's bomb'. The look she gave me." I shake my head. "I'm so stupid."

"So she knows that you know. Is she going to let you handle it?"

"No, she wants to handle it herself. I don't think I can convince her to let me help her. She's not going to trust me after today."

Richard pinches his lips together in thought, "Is she going to use it?"

"I don't think so."

"You don't think so?" He stands from his place at the table and begins to pace. "Is there any chance that she'll use it?"

I think for a long time. I know how irrational she can be. I remember my argument with Alec and my discussion with her. Richard stops pacing and makes eye contact with me.

"Maybe we should let her." he says after examining my face. I tilt my head in confusion.

"I'm sorry? You want her to detonate the bomb? That would kill all of these people. It would kill her!"

"Not if we evacuate everyone first. Listen, Nathan hasn't pitched finishing phase two to the government yet. All of the research needed is in this bunker and nowhere else. If we can destroy it with the bomb, which is the final piece. We can slow this whole operation down. Long enough to put an end to this. The East won't have to suffer the way we did."

"And Scarlet?"

"If you can get the bomb from her I may be able to put a timer on the bomb, giving her time to escape."

"Why does she have to be the one to do it?"

"She doesn't." He shrugs. "But from what you've said, I don't think she would let anyone else make that sacrifice. In her head, this is her battle not ours."

I bite my lower lip before saying, "How am I supposed to get my hands on it?"

"Ask her nicely."

I look down at my hands. This is nuts. She'd never let me take it from her and knowing Scarlet she would insist on pulling this stunt alone.

"Maybe the two of us could talk to her." I suggest.

"Set up a meeting and I'll be there." he agrees. I smile weakly at him and stand from my chair. I open my mouth to say one last thing, but no words form so I just nod and turn to leave.

Laura follows me to the door.

"Finn." I don't respond. "Finn." she repeats, grabbing my arm gently. I stop and turn to her, not meeting her gaze. "Honey, I know this is hard and I'm so sorry you and your friends are stuck in the middle."

"It's okay Laura."

She touches my cheek gently, "Are you okay?"

I shrug weakly.

"Don't shut down Finn, I know that's what you want. But you can't afford to do that now. Please let yourself feel, for your sake and for Scarlet's. If you want to save her," She moves her thumb gently along my cheek bone, "and I know that you do. You have to be present." I reach up and hold her hand to my cheek, closing my eyes and breathing deeply. A lump forms in my throat and my eyes fill with tears. I blink them away, shaking my head.

"You don't have to be strong in front of me." I raise my eyes to look at her. "You're my son. You can cry." I try my best to offer her a smile but I can't. My body shakes as she embraces me. I try to fight it, I don't want to be weak, but I don't know how to be strong now. I cry softly for a moment or two and then pull away.

"I have to go." I finally say.

She nods, "We're going to get through this. I love you Finn."

I force a weak smile and nod in return, turning to leave.

I walk through the hallway, my eyes on the floor.

* * *

The evening comes quickly. I have a meeting with Nathan tonight, though he's given me no clues as to what this is about. As I near his office my heart begins to pound against my chest, the same way it does everytime I'm close to him. Every time I meet with him, I wonder if I will walk out alive or be carried out in a body bag with a bullet hole in my forehead.

I don't bother knocking this time, the door is left slightly open.

"Finn," Nathan nods at me in a greeting, "How have you been doing?"

"I'm well Nathan." I respond, forcing myself to sound more confident than I actually am.

"Good. How is your mission going? Have we uncovered anything new about your friends?"

I shake my head, "No sir, no new information. They had a meeting a couple of days ago to discuss whether they should move on or not, but nothing suspicious was brought up."

"And are they going to move on?" He raises an eyebrow.

"No, they've decided to stay longer."

"Ah." He frowns, "And your girlfriend? Scarlet. Any updates

on her."

I swallow hard, why did he call her my girlfriend? My head spins as I momentarily forget to reply to him.

"No sir," I squeak, shaking my head, "I haven't seen much of her recently."

"So you aren't keeping close tabs on her? Is that what you're saying?"

I shake my head again.

"Because if she isn't with you, then who knows what she could be up to. Plotting maybe? You said in your reports that she was prone to that kind of behaviour. Am I wrong?"

"She's not plotting anything Nathan. She's just adjusting."

Nathan's eyes narrow as he studies me. Can he tell I'm lying? Probably. He's the one who taught me how to lie, and I never did master the skill. I find myself instinctively dropping my eyes to the floor. He huffs triumphantly.

"There's something that you are not telling me." He rests his elbows on the table, clasping his hands together and resting his chin on them. His eyes shift back and forth, scanning me. "We've talked about this Finn. I don't like being lied to."

"I'm not lying." I snap.

"Why so defensive?"

"Maybe because I don't like being accused, Nathan." I spit. "Scarlet is not plotting against you, but if she was I wouldn't blame her. You're a power hungry psychopath. Who gave you the right to—" I cut myself off. I watch Nathan's hand, fearing that it would go straight for the pistol in the left drawer of his desk. One shot, right in between my eyebrows and that would be it. Scarlet would truly be on her own.

"I'm sorry?" Nathan stands slowly from his seat. "I don't appreciate the name calling Finn, seems rather disrespectful, don't you think?"

"You don't deserve my respect." I swallow my fear and stand up. I'd never noticed before that I'm taller than him by a couple of inches. Compared to Nathan I've always felt small. He's not as powerful as he seems.

Nathan yawns, "I'll find out what she's planning one way or another. You know I will."

"If you go anywhere near her, you'll be seeing Carrie a lot sooner than you thought." I growl.

His hand goes for the pistol. Before I can think, I find myself diving over the desk, tackling him to the ground. He laughs in disbelief, the gun gripped tight in his right hand. I grab his wrist, slamming his hand into the floor until he releases his grip. His eyes grow wild with fear as I press the gun into his forehead. Fear, an emotion I was unaware that he had. I feel a grin spreading across my face, I have the power.

"You won't shoot me." he laughs through heavy breaths.

"Wanna bet?" My hand is surprisingly steady as my finger finds the trigger.

"Finn!" Laura startles me, running into the room. "What are you doing?"

I look at her.

Nathan uses the distraction to his advantage, his knee connects with my stomach, hard enough to make me roll off of him and onto the floor. He takes the gun from me as I cough, holding my stomach. I expect to feel a bullet ripping through my skull, but to my surprise, Nathan sets the gun down on the table. His eyes still locked on me, but the anger has dissipated slightly.

"That's what I thought." he chuckles. "You're just as weak as the day you started training. Your parents would be disappointed in the coward you've become." He smirks slightly and then turns to Laura. "Get him out of my office. We'll discuss this more later."

Laura helps me off of the floor and drags me out of Nathan's office, slamming the door behind us.

* * *

I glare at the floor as Laura marches us down the hallway. A small part of me can't help but feel triumphant, I've been dreaming of standing up to Nathan since my parents first sent me here. We come to my room. I open the door and walk to the bed without looking at Laura.

"Are you hurt?" she asks, her hands feeling over my face and arms for cuts or bumps.

I shake my head, "No, I'm not."

"What the hell was that?" she finally says after looking me over one more time. "Are you trying to get yourself killed?"

"I'm just so tired of being afraid of him Laura. He has my friend's lives in his maniacal hands. He has all the power and I hate it."

"But you have to play it smart Finn. You can't just lose it like that. He could have killed you, and then who would be protecting Scarlet? It sounds like your friends are ready to leave her here, you're her last hope. Are you willing to sacrifice her?"

"No." I choke out. Leave it to Laura to put these things into perspective. I should have controlled myself better. "But I had him. I could have pulled that trigger and—"

"And then what?"

"And then I would be the one with the power." I reply. "I wouldn't be helpless anymore because I would be the one calling the shots." I think for a moment.

"Finn…"

"No! Don't you get it? If he dies, we're the ones in control. We won't have to use the bomb, nobody else would get hurt. She would be safe along with everybody else."

"And when they send people to investigate why Nathan hasn't reached out? What then?"

"Once he's gone, we can leave."

"What about all of the plans? They would find them."

"We can collect them and burn them."

"We would never find them all. They'd make their way into the wrong hands eventually."

"Well there has to be a better option Laura. Something that puts an end to this and keeps Scarlet alive."

Laura stares at me for a long while, searching for something. Maybe just trying to find the right thing to say.

"What?" I finally ask her.

"Has it occurred to you that Scarlet doesn't want to be alive?"

"What does that mean?"

"It just seems like she doesn't. You need to consider the fact that she would rather do it the way Richard suggested."

"She isn't suicidal. She's just impulsive. She probably hasn't thought of another option. She doesn't *want* to die."

"Okay." she sighs., "I believe you."

"Do you?" I narrow my eyes. I can tell she doesn't

Laura pinches her lips together and nods slowly.

"So, can we meet with Richard about the plan?" I change the subject

"I'll talk to him, but I can't make you any promises. Honey, there just isn't enough time. We need to pull this off quick and get out of here."

"Why? What's the rush?"

"Cyrus is supposed to be meeting with Nathan sometime in the next month.

"Cyrus is coming here? That must mean that they're about to follow through with the rest of phase two."

Cyrus is Nathan's boss. He's the one that we turn all of our research in to. But we had assumed he wouldn't be back for a while since Evan destroyed our plans.

"Which means that Nathan finished the research." Laura says.

"No." I shake my head. "He doesn't have it yet. But he knows where he can get it."

"Scarlet." she confirms. Our panicked eyes meet. It takes everything in me to not cause a scene and run to Scarlet. I want to take her as far away from this place as I possibly can.

"You stay here." Laura walks towards the door. "I'll talk to Richard and see what he says." I nod, signalling that I agree to stay in my room until she returns. "I'm serious Finn. Do not go after him, stay here until we can figure something out."

"I won't." I reply.

I flop down on the bed once she's gone. Taking deep breaths to calm myself. I close my eyes and shortly after, find myself drifting into a shallow sleep.

* * *

The past few days have been filled with me keeping my head

down and trying to negotiate a new plan with Richard and Laura. Richard is convinced that his way is the only way, his pride is going to get us all killed. Nathan hasn't asked for a meeting with me yet, I've been waiting for something... anything to happen. If I wasn't close with Laura, I would have been executed by now. Even though I am important to her, I'm surprised I'm still alive after attacking him like that.

Richard and I have been sitting at his table since early this morning trying to come to an agreement.

"This is the best way to be sure everything is destroyed before Cyrus gets here." Richard argues. "His last message suggests he'll be here within the week."

"You can't just sacrifice Scarlet like this Richard. You and I both know there's a better way to go about this. If you'd just let me get my hands on him." I squeeze Nathan's imaginary neck, "We can end this and be gone before Cyrus gets here."

"It isn't that simple and you know it."

"It is that simple Richard. Nobody else has to die."

"I keep telling you that if you could get your hands one the bomb, I can set a timer on it."

"Why do we have to use the bomb at all?"

"It's the only way to be sure all of the research is destroyed." he replies. He pauses to take a deep breath before saying, "Look, I told you. I will do it, it doesn't have to be Scarlet but you know better than I do that she won't go for it."

"I can't lose her Richard." I swallow. "She's the only thing keeping me going."

"Then get her in here to talk to me. I will take her place if she'll hand over the bomb." he replies, placing his hand on my shoulder and squeezing gently.

"Okay. I'll try. Give me a day."

"That's all we have left to spare." he tells me, "We may not even have that."

I nod and stand, pushing my chair away from the table.

"Work fast Finn. We can't afford to be too late."

16

Scarlet

It's been days and Alec still isn't speaking to me. I can't blame him really. In a way I put them in danger as much as I put myself in danger. Or maybe it is just that he does care.

Things have changed between Shark and I. He doesn't seem angry, maybe a little disappointed. I haven't brought up anything about the bomb since Shark talked about sneaking it out of my room. I haven't even looked at it since that day.

At this time I'm helping Ally get ready for her date with Sam. She's so excited. I'm glad we stayed, even if it was just for Ally's happiness.

"How's this?" she asks me, she walks out of the bathroom. The dress is simple. Dark blue and flowy. Her reddish brown hair is down. I don't think I've ever seen her wear it like that, it makes her look older.

"Where'd you get the dress?" I ask curiously.

"Sam's friend Jenna lent it to me. Isn't it pretty?"

"You look beautiful Ally, really." I smile. I know Alec isn't the biggest fan of his young niece going out with a boy, but even without him talking to me, I know we both agree that it's great seeing her happy.

"Okay, get out, he'll be here any-'' She's interrupted by a knock. "Shoot, never mind." She opens the door. She smiles at me.

"You look amazing!" I hear Sam say. "You ready?"

I watch Ally grab his hand, allowing him to lead her out the door.

I clean her room up a little before leaving. I find myself wandering towards the library. That seems to be the place I've been hanging out in the most at this point. I don't really read, but I love the quiet atmosphere. It comforts me in a way.

I walk down the hallway in some kind of a daze. Once again, I am on autopilot, allowing my legs to lead me wherever.

"Scarlet." I look up to realize I almost walked right into Doctor Fowler.

"Oops. Sorry." I apologize flatly. I walk past him and continue on my way to the library.

"You know Scarlet."

I freeze, keeping my back to him.

"It took me a while to realize who you are."

"Who I am?" I ask confused.

"Yes, Kat talked about you quite a bit while she was staying with us." A chill makes its way through my body. "Of course I recognized Reese immediately, but it took some time for me to realize Kevin was here as well, Ty too. But no Kat?" I ball my hands into fists and clench my teeth. Don't cry, not in front of him. "Where is she? I wouldn't mind getting to catch up with her." His tone is menacing.

Kat's suicide plays through my memory again. Flashes of her blood, her eyes, the *bang* of the gun. I blink tears out of my eyes and turn to face the doctor.

"Oh." He suppresses a laugh after reading my expression. "My condolences." he says unsympathetically.

"What do you want, Doctor?" I ask as calmly as I can.

"Never mind Kat, I suppose she's paid for what she's done." He steps closer to me. "And don't worry, you and your friends will be safe here. As long as you don't go and shoot anyone else that is." Our eyes challenge each other as they do every time we encounter one another.

I begin to turn to walk away.

"And." he says. I keep walking, but slower. "You tell me exactly what Evan told you about the bunkers." I swallow hard, freezing mid-step. What does he know about Evan?

"Evan?" I'll pretend I don't know anything.

"Yes, Evan. I know he was a part of your group at one time or another. We wouldn't have let a bomb tech run away without some way to keep an eye on him, especially not our best bomb tech."

"Bomb tech?" I mumble to myself. That explains so much about Evan. "Evan was telling the truth..."

"Yes, Evan told your group too much of the truth. But my source informed me that he may have told *you* even more." Without warning Doctor Fowler grabs my wrist. I inhale sharply, my heart beats hard and fast. I remember Evan grabbing my wrists and I instantly feel like I'm in danger. Am I panicking? I feel like I might pass out.

"Your source?"

"Yes, my source; Finn." He grips my wrist tighter. I wince slightly. "I believe you know him well."

"I don't know a Finn." I glare at him. What is he talking about? A spy? Following Evan? What are they hiding? What does he think I know?

"Your boyfriend." he whispers in my ear. What? Shark? No, I would've known.

"You're lying." I accuse him. There's no way. I think through the last few months.

"Go ahead." He finally lets go of me. Whether it's fear or what, I'm frozen. "Ask him." Doctor Fowler walks calmly away, as if we didn't just have the conversation we just had. I let out a breath I was holding in and rub my wrist, wincing again. I forgot how much that hurts. "There's no way..." I say to myself.

I find myself running to Shark's room and banging on the door.

"What?!" I hear him shout. "I'm coming hold on!" I keep knocking anyway. He opens the door, his eyes grow wide as I shove past him and slam the door.

"Finn?" I feel lied to, betrayed. It makes sense now. The close attention he paid to Evan. Him going on about how he needed to leave, he had something he had to do. It all makes sense.

"You're a spy?!"

His jaw drops open, he wasn't expecting me to find out. Why did Fowler tell me? "All this time, you were spying on us, for them? Was everything a lie?" I pause for a breath.

He opens his mouth to speak, but I raise my hand signaling him to remain silent.

"I trusted you Shark, we all did! You're telling me everything Evan said was true, and you knew, and you lied about it? I can't believe I let myself fall in love with you. I let myself trust you. And all this time, you were on their side?" I would cry right now but not in front of him. I don't trust him with that anymore.

"Scarlet, it's not like that. I do love you. You *can* trust me."

He steps towards me, I back away. I begin to laugh hysterically. I actually thought he was good, the best actually.

"How? How am I supposed to trust you now? I don't think I can. I didn't even know your name!"

"You can." he replies. "I won't tell them about the bomb. I haven't. I promise. I'll get rid of it, like I said. You'll be safe, you'll all be safe and we can be together. That doesn't have to change." I forgot he knew about the bomb. What if he's lying? What if they already know?

"No, the bomb stays where it is." I say. "And you and I cannot be together. You work for *them*. They killed my family. You helped them do it. You're just as bad as Evan." I subconsciously touch my wrist.

I follow his eyes to the bruising forming on my wrist.

"No. You don't get to freak out over that." I tell him.

"He hurt you." Shark mumbles.

"Not as much as you did." I reply, my voice low. I walk out of his room feeling more vulnerable than before.

I trusted him, loved him. I feel threatened. He knows everything about me and now there's a good chance Doctor Fowler does too.

I find myself panicking, wondering what else they know. Do they think I'm a threat? Are we actually safe? Do I tell the others? As much as I want to hate him, as much as I want Alec to kill him right now. I can't bring myself to do it. Even knowing this, I can't do that to him. I tell myself I'll keep his secret.

I forget about my outing to the library and go back to my room and I don't leave for days.

* * *

"Scarlet?" Ally knocks on my door, as she's done once an hour for the last three days. "Scarlet, I don't know what's going on. But I'm here for you if you want to talk. You know that right?" A pause. "You have to know that."

I haven't felt like talking to people since I found out about Finn.

I've gotten myself used to calling him Finn, Shark just doesn't feel right anymore.

I loved Shark. Finn is a liar.

I haven't eaten in three days. I've only slept, and cried. I've pulled the bomb out a few times, wondering if I'd given up on my mission too early. I keep considering blowing this place and myself up.

"Scarlet, come on. You can't stay in there forever. You need food and hugs. I have hugs." Ally is still calling to me through the door. "Kevin's here too."

"Hey Scarlet, how ya doin' in there?" I hear Kevin say.

"Oh come on you can do better than that." I hear Ally say to him.

"Whattya want me to do? Kick the door down?" he replies. I can picture them considering it.

"You don't have to kick the door down stupid. They don't lock." I hear Ally say. I bury myself under the blankets, preparing myself for them to just barge in.

"Oh yeah." Kevin chuckles. I watch as the door knob turns and the two of them walk cautiously inside.

"What's up Scarlet?" Kevin asks, sitting on the floor by the bed. Ally sits on the edge of the bed and rubs my back. I grumble incoherent words.

"What's going on? We haven't seen you in days." Ally asks. What am I supposed to tell them? I sit up and look at Ally. My eyes tear up. "Oh Scarlet, what happened?" She looks at Kevin confused. He shrugs. I lean into her shoulder, she hugs me tight and I cry. Kevin and Ally begin to cry with me.

We cry for a long time. By the end my eyes are red and puffy and my throat is dry.

"I'm sorry guys." I sniffle.

"It's okay." Ally wipes her eyes. "I think we all needed that."

"Are you okay though?" Kevin asks.

"No." I admit.

"What can we do?" Ally holds my hand. I look between the two of them and then I force a small smile.

"Why don't you tell me how your date went?" I suggest. "I haven't heard yet."

"Okay." She squeezes my hand and begins telling me all about her day with Sam. It sounds like they had a lot of fun.

I find myself growing jealous, seeing how my relationship ended, but I'm so glad she's happy with him. She deserves that much.

I sit quietly and listen, giggling every now and then.

"I'm really happy for you Ally." I tell her. I smile easier now.

"Thanks." She smiles shyly, her cheeks turning bright red for a second.

"Scarlet..." She pinches her lips together, trying to decide if she should ask or not.

"I don't want to talk about it." I answer the question she didn't ask. Her and Kevin lock eyes again.

"Okay." She sighs. "At Least come to dinner please. You can't starve yourself."

"I don't know Ally." I frown. I'm not ready to face Finn right now.

"He won't be there." Kevin tells me, as if he could read my

mind. "Shark hasn't been at any meals either." Why? What is it he has to be upset about? I nod reluctantly and lead the way to the dining hall.

They were right, he isn't here. I can't help but feel disappointed, feel like I've lost something. I scan the room multiple times for him. I don't see him, but my eyes find their way to Doctor Fowler. Christopher stands beside him as they talk to Richard and Laura.

My throat grows tight for a moment as our eyes meet from across the room. He smirks. *"You don't scare me."* I think, hoping he can somehow hear my thoughts.

I smile at him and challenge him with my eyes until he finally looks away. Returning his full attention to his family.

I turn to leave the line, my nearly empty plate in hand.

"Would you watch it?" Alec grumbles as I accidentally bump into him. I manage to keep my food from spilling on him as I regain my balance. I ignore him and begin to walk towards the tables.

"Oh gosh Alec, I'm so sorry. Didn't see ya there." I hear him mocking me quietly. I bite my tongue, hoping it will be enough to keep me from getting into yet another argument.

"I'd love to apologize." I turn back to him. He gestures to me, awaiting my apology. "I'd love to apologize. But I'm not sorry." I turn once again and walk to the nearest empty place, setting my plate down.

Kevin and Ally begin to join me, but I hear a grunt. Which I assume was Alec signaling them to sit somewhere else. He sits across the table from me and watches me eat my three bites.

"What Alec?" I growl. Scraping my fork around my plate. "Here to yell at me some more."

"Where have you been?" he asks. His voice is calm.

"Locked in my room."

"Got anything to do with that?" He points to my wrist. "You gotta stop making people mad." he mutters.

Instinctively, I hide it under the table. I look up to see Doctor Fowler has left. Should I tell Alec? Should I trust Alec? I don't want to do that to Shark...or Finn I guess.

I still love him for some reason. I can't bring myself to rat him out.

"It's nothing Alec." I look down, ashamed. "You know me, picking fights I could never win."

He stares at me for a long while.

"You gonna tell me?" He finally speaks again.

"Why should I?" I mumble.

"Scarlet, you and I rarely get along. I'm still not really sure if I even like you. I definitely don't trust your judgement. But, if somebody's threatening you, I want to know."

"I can handle it Alec."

"No, you obviously can't" He rolls his eyes and begins to stand up. "Whatever, get yourself killed. I don't care."

"Wait Alec." I want to tell him. I want to tell somebody. He waits for me to say more. "Evan was right." I just can't let him walk away still thinking I'm crazy. I need him to know Evan was right. My judgement wasn't off.

He glares at me, "Scarlet, I really don't want to go over this again right now."

"Evan was right." I raise my wrist slightly. "He knew everything. Doctor Fowler knows I know."

Alec thinks for a moment.

"Does that change things?" I know he's asking if that I've changed my mind about the bomb. In all honestly, it has crossed my mind, but I don't know. I need to learn more. I look at him, but I don't reply.

"I don't know why I keep trying."

"I have to do something. He can't just get away with it."

"Do whatever Scarlet." He sighs. He looks defeated. If I didn't know better, I'd think he may be hurt. "I'm done."

My blood goes cold. Of course we fight all of the time, but this felt different. It felt final. And to think the two of us had almost built a friendship. I watch him walk away, slower than usual. Sadder than usual.

Ally and Kevin follow him out. I wonder what he'll tell them. Will he tell them anything? Would he turn them against me?

"Scarlet!" Christopher comes skipping up to me once the others have left the cafeteria.

"Now's not the best time kid." I grumble.

"Are you okay?" he asks. "I haven't seen ya in days." He ignores my tone.

"Yeah. I'm fine."

"Your boyfriend's been spending a lot of time with me uncle. He's super cool ya know. Smart too." he tells me.

"Oh yeah?" I reply, my voice flat. Should hearing him refer to Finn as "my boyfriend" hurt this much? Like being stabbed in the stomach? More accurately, the back.

Should this pain of losing Shark hurt more than any other pain I've felt in the last few months? Even more than Kat's death. Maybe not, but it does.

"He asked me about you." Christopher continues to talk. "Wondered how you've been. Said he hasn't seen ya in a couple days." I smile at the boy. Should I play along? Ask him to tell Shark I'm doing well maybe?

"I'm sure he did." I reply, trying to sound as friendly as possible.

"My uncle had him moved into one of the military suites. They're much nicer. He really likes him."

"I'm sure he likes that." I stand up from my seat. I want to tell Christopher to say hi to him for me, I want to ask him where his room is. I wonder if maybe I owe it to Shark to let him explain.

As hurt as I am, I still want to believe he is who he was before. I want to think he's still caring and protective of me. I still want to believe he's goofy and romantic. But I can't.

"See ya kid." I walk out of the cafeteria and return to my room, feeling worse than before.

17

Shark

If Scarlet won't let me take the bomb to protect her, then I need to think of a different approach. I find myself walking towards Nathan's office, my heart beating so fast I think I might pass out. I rehearse every word I'll say as I near the room. I tell myself I'll apologize and ask forgiveness. I'll tell him I'm committed to him and the mission and I'm ready to get serious. I have to get into his inner circle again.

I knock once, too quiet for a human to hear. I swallow and breathe. I knock again, louder this time.

"Come in." he calls from the other side of the door. Slowly I open the door and step into his office. Anger slowly creeps into his eyes as I sit myself down across from him.

"Finn." He acknowledges me.

"Nathan." I greet him shyly, the boldness I'd built up in the hallway suddenly gone.

"I didn't think I'd be seeing you back in here anytime soon." he says, scanning me up and down. "Bold."

"Nathan..." I begin, "I'm sorry."

"Sorry." He lets out a short, humorless laugh. "You held a

gun to my head Finn. You threatened my life."

"I'm here to apologize. It got out of hand, it won't happen again sir, I promise. I lost sight of my job but I'm ready to get back to my mission now."

"So, you want me to put you back on the mission, after you sabotaged it for the girl that's trying to sabotage me." We study each other in silence for a moment. "Ah, I get it. She found out. Didn't she?"

"Yes." I swallow. Lying to Nathan will only make this more difficult.

"And she left you. I'm all you have to turn to." He grins.

I nod cautiously. He chuckles, an evil grin spreading across his face.

"I could use your knowledge of the group," he says. "But I'll be moving you to the military dorms. I can't risk you being so close to Scarlet again. I don't trust you won't betray me for her again." He glares at me.

"So then how do you plan for me to continue my mission? They'll become suspicious if I suddenly stop staying in the guest bunks."

"I don't need you to be close to them anymore. I know everything I need to."

I study his demonic expression for a long moment before replying, "What do you know?" I ask cautiously, fearful that I may have reignited any suspicions he has of me.

He cocks his head slightly, "I know that you lied to me about Scarlet. You told me she wasn't planning anything. She was harmless." he scoffs. "But I know that she has my bomb and I need it before Cyrus gets here next week."

"Cyrus will be here next week. At least that gives me a little time." I think. "Why don't you just take it?" I ask. "If you know that

she has it."

"Because once I find the bomb, I will be obligated to kill her and to be completely honest with you Finn, I love watching that girl fall apart." A shiver makes its way up my spine, I fight the urge you shake it out of my body. "But time is running out. Cyrus and his team need the bomb to approve the rest of phase two."

"Nathan," I pause for a moment to reevaluate the question I'm about to ask. "Forgive me for asking, but before I fully recommit to this, I just need to know, Why is finishing phase two *so* important?"

Nathan glares at me and for a moment I think he may be about to jump over the desk and grab my neck, but he only sighs and looks at the picture of his wife.

"Because of overpopulation Finn, you know why."

"Haven't we've killed enough people to solve that problem? At least for a long while." I argue.

"Do you know what it's like to lose control Finn? To watch somebody you love, die in a pool of their own blood?" He gives me no time to respond. "This bomb gives me the power to control who lives and dies. I'm in control now. In this bunker, I am king. If this plan falls through and I don't have the bomb when Cyrus comes, I lose my kingdom. But, if we finish phase 2 and 'save the planet' I get to stay on my throne. I'm not willing to give this up, not while I have the power to make sure that your friends don't make it out of here alive."

"This is all about power?"

"If you back out now, I can assure you that your dear Scarlet's death will be prolonged and painful." He smirks. I feel myself begin to sweat, as much as I wish my fear of him would disappear. I swallow hard, weighing my options. Either I back out and try to get Scarlet out of here as fast as I can, or I follow Nathan's lead until I can think of a better plan.

"Are you with me? Or should I make a trip to the guest dorms?"

"I'm with you." I choke out.

"Then start moving your stuff and meet Richard and I back here for breakfast." He orders.

"Yes sir." I reply as I stand and turn to leave his office.

I hurry back to my dorm to get my stuff, keeping my head down in the hopes that I won't run into Scarlet. Even though I don't believe I have to worry about it, Scarlet hasn't left her room since she'd learned who I really was. I don't blame her. When I arrive at my room, Laura is waiting for me. I make eye contact with her as I close the door.

"Why?" she begins. "You should never have gone back to him Finn!"

"How did you—"

"It is my job to know! You are my son, I know when you're in danger. I know when you do something stupid! He could have shot you the moment you walked through his door? Are you trying to kill yourself?"

"He didn't shoot me." I argue. "I did what I had to, to keep Scarlet safe."

"You can't keep her safe if you're dead! How many times am I going to have to say that to you?" she shouts.

"Would you stop yelling at me?" I snap. "I'm just trying to keep everyone safe. I don't *want* to work for Nathan again. He terrifies me. But losing Scarlet, scares me even more. Look, I know that Scarlet doesn't want—" I have to stop myself before I let the words slip from my tongue, "I just have to keep her safe." I finally say. "I'll be careful, I promise. I just...I need to at least try to save her."

"I know you do." She smiles weakly, her anger dissipating

"I'm just not sure she'll ever trust me again." I drop my gaze to the floor.

"Of course she will, she loves you."

"No Laura, she loves Shark. She loves that man who I pretended to be those months at the house. She hates Finn, who I really am. A coward, a follower. I followed Nathan's plan blindly and it cost me her trust, it cost me myself. How can she love me Laura? How could anybody? I helped murder so many people, and until I got to know her, I didn't even realize it was wrong."

"I think you have it backwards." she replies.

"What do you mean?"

"The 'Finn' you described is not who you are. You love fiercely. You would do anything for those you love. I'll admit that before you left to track down Evan, I'd thought that part of you was slipping away. That Nathan's influence has begun to corrupt your golden heart. But seeing you with this group, seeing you with Scarlet has proven me wrong." She steps closer to me, placing her hand on my cheek. "I hate that you don't love who you are and that all you see is a coward, because that isn't who you are. I love you so much Finn and Scarlet still loves you." Her voice shakes as tears form in her eyes.

"I love you too." I finally say. "But I'm afraid Scarlet may never feel that way again and who could blame her? I lied to her about everything."

Laura opens her mouth but then shakes her head, as if to change her mind, "Richard wants word with you once you're settled into your new room."

"Okay, I'll come by in half an hour." I tell her. She blinks the tears from her eyes, studying me. She pulls me into a gentle hug, holding me for a long moment before pulling away. I busy myself with packing up my limited amount of belongings, not acknowledging her as she leaves the room. I push my thoughts out of my head and focus everything on packing.

* * *

The days leading to Cyrus' arrival go by slowly. Each day I meet with Nathan, It seems to be his way of watching me. So he can be sure I'm not sneaking off to inform Scarlet of his plans. I haven't seen her or the others in a a few days. It's strange to spend everyday with certain people and then suddenly not see them anymore. After I meet with Nathan in the mornings, I sneak off to Richards room. He still hasn't been able to speak with Scarlet about our plans and time is running out. Although lately, Nathan has kept Richard and I in the dark on when Cyrus is coming, we assume it will be in the next couple of days.

"Well my dear Finn." Nathan begins our meeting, today Richard sits beside me across from Nathan. "Tomorrow is the day."

"The day?" I ask, although I already know what he means. Today is the day he collects the bomb. His toying with Scarlet and watching her fall apart has come to an end.

"You know what day." he laughs. "Cyrus comes in two days, which means that I'm going to need that bomb today."

"I'll go get it for you." I offer. I feel Richard glancing at me from the corner of my eye.

"No, I'd like to do this myself." He smirks. "It's been a while since I've seen Scarlet, it would be nice to catch up with her."

"What do you plan to do with the girl Nathan?" Richard asks. I sigh in relief, grateful that I wan't the one to ask. I think I already know the answer but Nathan can be unpredictable.

"I haven't fully decided." Nathan's eyes meet with mine. "I won't hurt her today though, not if I don't have to. But there must be some form of punishment for bringing such a threat within our borders. With the intent to kill. I can't simply forgive that kind of thing, you know that."

"I'm sure you'll think of something." I respond, narrowing my eyes.

"Oh I most certainly will." he growls. The gleam in his eye gives me goose bumps. Who finds this much joy in ruining peoples lives?

"Is that all you wanted us for Nathan?" Richard asks impatiently.

"It is. I thought you would be excited. We've almost completely phase two and by the end of this week not only will our plans be approved, but I'll be down one major annoyance in my life. What a wonderful week it will be."

Richard and I exchange a look and rise from our seats.

"Finn, I'll see you in the lab after lunch." Nathan says. I nod, signaling that I heard him. I'm fearful of what he could possibly have to show me then. But I assume it has something to do with Scarlet and the bomb.

Outside of the room, five of the bunkers guards are waiting to be let into Nathan's office. I hold the door, eyeing each one as they file into the room.

I close the door and stand staring down the hallway, wondering what my next move should be.

"Finn." Richard touches my shoulder. "You have go."

"Go?" I reply, hardly listening.

"To Scarlet." he says calmly. "Get the bomb and get her out of here, this is our last chance. If Nathan gets the bomb, it's over. We can't save her and we can't stop the attacks."

I continue to stare down the hallway. Attempting to process our conversation. I knew that this day was coming and I knew that it would be soon. But I was frozen. For the last time I have to decide what I want to do. Do I go against Nathan and save Scarlet? Do I give the bomb to Richard or take it and run?

"Now Finn!" Richard shakes me urgently. I take off sprinting through the halls towards Scarlet's room. My mind void of everything but her name and the feeling that I have to get to her.

18

Scarlet

I've lost track of the days once again. I leave my room every now and then to get food, but that's about all I've been doing. I haven't run into Alec or Finn at all. It's crossed my mind that maybe Alec and the other's have packed up and gone back to the house. I wouldn't blame them if they did.

Christopher has stopped by every now and then, updating me on Shark's status, telling me all about how close he's gotten with Doctor Fowler and how he asks of me often.

I spend most of my spare time thinking. Sometimes I remember the days back at Alec's. Strange to think that things seemed simpler then.

I remember when Shark took me on that date. Back before I knew. I keep thinking back through every conversation we've had together, looking through my memory for signs. Searching for missed signals. I should have seen it, I should have known.

I think about Evan often, I feel guilty for his death now. Now that I know he was right. Would Finn have killed him anyway? Did he really kill him to protect me or was it part of his mission? I guess I'll never know.

Knowing Evan was right caused me to reconsider the bomb, as Alec already knew I would. I know it's not the right answer. Not everyone in this bunker deserves to die, only the ones directly responsible.

It's crazy to think that I may be the one who's able to do it. But not until I know what they're hiding, not until I can be sure they have nothing else up their sleeves. I sit on my bed like this for hours. Staring angrily at the door. Plotting.

A knock breaks me out of my thoughts. It startles me slightly, it's not time for Christopher to be knocking and I haven't heard from the other's since Alec and I last talked.

I wonder if Shark finally caved and told Doctor Fowler about Evan's bomb. A second knock. No if they were here for the bomb, I'd be dead already.

Slowly I walk to the door, opening it just enough for me to see Finn standing outside. He's wearing a suit now, white and clean, like what I often see Richard wearing.

Why is he here? Maybe he's gonna turn me in himself.

"No." I say, closing the door.

"Scarlet, we need to talk." he says through the door. I open it again.

"I don't want to talk." I reply. I begin to close the door a second time, but he pushes it the rest of the way open. "I didn't say come in." I try to push him back out. My efforts are useless seeing as I'm less than half his size.

"This is important." he says. He comes the rest of the way into the room, closing the door gently behind him. "We have to be fast. He could be here any minute."

"Finn..." His name feels weird on my tongue. "I really don't want to hear it."

"You have to." He grabs my shoulders aggressively. I flinch a bit, but I don't feel threatened. As much as I don't trust him, I know he wouldn't hurt me. "Listen, you have to get out of here. I know you don't trust me, and you don't have to. But Scarlet, you have to run."

"Why?" I don't understand what he's trying to warn me of. "You tell him about the bomb?"

"No." He suddenly begins whispering. "I wouldn't put you in that much danger. Scarlet, Nathan has his own way of finding things out and not only does he know you have the bomb, but he needs the bomb."

"Why"

"I don't have the time to explain Scarlet, please just trust me."

"What is it that this man is hiding?" I ask. "Do you know?"

He nods, his eyes drifting to the floor.

"Finn." I step closer to him, I have to know what he knows. His hands release their grip on my shoulders. "Shark." He looks back up at me. His expression softer than before, like the man I knew before I met Finn. "How can you expect me to trust you, if you won't tell me what's going on?"

"It doesn't matter. You can't do anything to stop him. All you can do is run, right now. Before he kills you." I search his eyes. Why would he lie to me about this? What would he gain from doing that?

"This doesn't make sense. He promised we'd be safe. You promised we'd be safe. What changed?" I think for a moment.

"He lied. Nathan lives to hurt people." he tells me. "Where are the others? You all need to be long gone by tomorrow."

"I don't know." I reply. "I figured they were already gone."

"I have to get back." he mumbles, looking at the watch on

211

his wrist. "Find them and run." He turns to leave.

"What about the bomb?" I ask. "Do I just leave it behind?"

"Will you let me take it?" he asks doubtfully. I shake my head, I still refuse to trust him with that.

"Then take it with you. You can't just leave it here. That would give him too much power."

"So...is this goodbye then?" I can't help but feel sad. He gives me a sad smile and walks out the door. I glance at the bomb one more time. If I was gonna blow something up, now would be the time. I shake the idea out of my head and focus myself on finding Alec and the others. They must still be here. Finn would've known if they left.

Not long after Finn leaves, Christopher comes to get me for dinner. I cut off his greeting.

"Have you seen my friends Chris?" I ask him. He thinks hard for a long moment.

"They were all headed to Alec's room a moment ago." he tells me. I push him out of the way in a more aggressive manner than I had intended.

"Sorry." I mutter as I walk swiftly in the direction of Alec's room. Quietly I knock on the door, paranoid that somebody may be watching.

"Not now Christopher." Alec calls through the door. I knock again, no answers. I bite my lower lip as I consider letting myself in. Remembering that we don't have the time for me to be scared, I turn the knob and slide into the room as quietly as I can.

"Scarlet." Ally greets me. She's not quite nice, but not hostile either. I turn to see the group spread out around the room. Alec is leaning against the wall, looking away from me.

"Look, I know I'm the last person you want to see right now. But we have to get out of here." I try to keep my voice as quiet as I can.

"What? Why?" Ally asks. Her voice trembles slightly. I assume she's thinking of Sam now.

"It's not safe. Doctor Fowler is planning something for tomorrow and if we want to live, we need to not be here."

"I told you we weren't safe." Reese speaks up. Ty elbows her side. "What?" she grumbles.

"Scarlet, now really isn't a good time for your drama." Alec says, walking towards me. "We're in the middle of a *team* meeting." He opens the door.

"No. I promise I'm not making this up." I back away from him, further into the room. "I'm being serious. Finn he...he came to my room. He told me that the Doctor knows about the bomb and we need to go, now.."

"Finn?" Kevin asks. "Who's Finn?"

"It doesn't matter." I sigh. I don't have time to tell them everything. "What matters now is that you guys make it out of here alive."

"Oh, now you're worried about that." Alec rolls his eyes.

"Alec, she's not lying." Kevin stands up and moves in between us. "Can't you see she's genuinely scared?"

"How do I know this isn't just your way of getting us out of here so you can blow this thing up?" Alec asks.

"You'll just have to trust me." I raise my voice. "Guys, I know I've messed up a lot lately. I know I don't deserve your trust. But I'm serious about this. If we don't leave right now, we will die."

"Well...you heard her." Alec sighs. His tone softened. "Pack up, we're leaving."

I sigh in relief. I nod to him, thanking him for trusting me. He looks away from me.

"Well, that was dramatic." Doctor Fowler's voice startles me. I watch as he comes into view from around the corner. "You know, if you plan on having a secret meeting, a good rule of thumb would be to close your door. Wouldn't want the wrong people to hear you."

I step in front of the doctor. Glaring at him as if it will do us any good.

"Doctor." I growl.

"Hey." He peeks his head back out the door and around the corner. "Would you please stop talking and arrest them already?"

Immediately following, a dozen or so men flood the room handcuffing everyone. Alec and Kevin put up a bit of a fight, but they're no match for the guards dragging them out of the room. I'm frozen, my mind races as I try to think of what to do next. Doctor Fowler closes the door once the other's are gone, leaving us alone.

I back away to the farthest wall. I don't want to be afraid, but I can't help it now. I'm cornered.

"You're not the brightest, are you?" He takes a step. "Hiding a bomb in your room? Did you think we wouldn't find out?" Another step. "Here I thought you may be a threat to my operation." Another step. What do I do? "Silly of me to be threatened by a child." Another step towards me.

"If you aren't threatened, why don't you just let us leave?" I ask him, barely able to get a breath out.

"As nice as that would be, I can't." Another step towards me. "Scarlet, I'm under the impression that you may know more than you should and while it is highly unlikely that you could pass that information off to someone who matters. I can't take that chance."

"We don't know anything."

"I know what Evan told you, I don't know what all Finn has told you, but I can't let you go out there with any information about our plans." Another step. "And either way, I'm not a big fan of you bringing a bomb into my home. You didn't think I would actually let you leave. After Kat killed my wife? After you planned to slaughter my people?" I can feel his breath on my face. My body is pressed as far into the wall as it will go. My heart pounds, waiting for him to do something. Suddenly he grabs my throat. His grip is tight. "I really like you Scarlet, you're spunky, bold. You've got potential. Too bad you're on the wrong side of this. I could have used that ruthlessness on my team."

After a couple of minutes pass he lets go of me. I gasp for air as I crumble to the floor.

"I'll have to thank you for bringing Evan's bomb back to us though. Now we can complete phase 2."

"Complete?" I repeat. What does that mean?

He sighs. I look up at him, afraid he's going to attack me again. He thinks for a moment.

"Well, we're going to kill you today anyway." He smiles slightly. "Might as well show you the operation. Come on." He grabs my upper arm and pulls me up off the floor. I feel weak, my head pounds as my lungs work hard to make up for lost breaths.

Doctor Fowler drags me out of the room and down to the last door at the end of the hall. It leads to a stairwell that I didn't know existed. We descend the stairs and enter some sort of high tech lab. Full of computers and test areas.

"Welcome to the lab." He grins. "This is where young Evan spent most of his time perfecting his bomb. Evan was a genius you know, our best tech. Of course we have hundreds of intelligent engineers working for us. None of them were able to mass produce a bomb that would cover more area than anything we've ever seen before, as well as ensuring that there are no survivors. You see, the bombs we used in these western states, they were average and they obviously missed a few people. The bomb Evan was working on contained a chemical that would infect survivors, slowly killing them. It was genius."

"That's horrible." I gasp.

"I know, it sounds bad." he replies. "But if we don't finish phase two, things will get much worse. I didn't think we'd be able to pull it off after Evan ran off with his research, after Finn neglected to finish his mission. I didn't think we'd have the missing piece. So Scarlet I would like to thank you. Thank you for bringing it back to us. Now within the next week we will truly have saved the nation from the trials of overpopulation."

"Haven't you done enough?"

"Not nearly." I watch as a tall and muscular man comes into the lab carrying my backpack, filled with Evan's plans and most importantly his bomb.

Is this bomb infused with whatever Evan was experimenting with? Is this one of those bombs? Fowler takes the bag from the man.

"Thank you. Would you kindly escort Scarlet to the others?" he asks the man. The man nods, Grabbing onto my arm. I want to fight him, to yell, scream. But what good will that do? We lost. I lost.

19

Shark

"Richard! He's got Scarlet and the bomb." I inform Richard as I run into their room, neglecting to knock before barging in. "The others are in the cell upstairs. You have to help me, it can't end like this."

"What did you have in mind Finn? Cyrus will be here in two days. You think Nathan is going to let us get to the bomb now?"

"We have to try. I told her to run, like you said. I ran to her and warned her, but he must have followed me there."

"Finn." Laura says coming out from their bedroom. "What more can we do? We've run out of time."

Richard types out something on his watch before looking back up at us. "If we move now, we may both get what we want." he finally says. "We can save your friends and destroy the bunker before Cyrus arrives."

"No, Richard, we didn't have the time to rig a timer or convince her to let one of us do it."

"You ran out of time Finn. You had all the time in the world to get that bomb from her and you failed." Richard snaps. "Our only hope of putting an end to this is go through with the plan the way we talked about before."

"No." I find myself stepping into Richards space until his back is to the wall. I tower over him. "We can't risk her life like this."

"Boys!" Laura shouts. "We don't have time for this."

"I've already dispatched a team of rogue soldiers to evacuate the bunker. You and I need to find Scarlet and that bomb while Nathan is distracted."

"Richard..." I want to argue but I fear that if I don't follow his lead I'll lose them all, not just Scarlet but everyone else that I love. I back away from him and nod, leading the way to the door.

* * *

"The guards are sneaking people out the side entrance, hopefully we have enough time to evacuate everyone before those loyal to Nathan come after us." Richard tells me. The two of us sprint down the hall, making it to the stairwell that goes up to the jail cell. "The bomb is going to be in the lab downstairs. Lead her to it Finn, finish this."

"She's not going to make it out of this if I take her down there."

"We don't have another option Finn, this is it. Either we do this now, or we become responsible for a million more deaths."

"This isn't our only option and you know it!"

"If Cyrus gets his hands on this research, it's over for us. The research will be in every bunker in the country. Do you have the fire power to destroy a hundred and twenty bunkers?"

I glare at him. I know that there's another way to end this, there has to be.

"You get her out of here, and I'll set off the bomb. I'll sacrifice myself."

"You know she won't go for that." he argues.

"Then drag her out of here Richard! I don't care how she gets out of here but it will not be a puff of smoke."

He thinks for a long moment, "No." he finally says.

"No." I repeat, laughing a weak, unamused laugh.

"Laura and I can't lose you." he protests.

"And I can't lose her."

I freeze when I hear the sound of people fighting coming from above us. Richard leans into the stairwell to listen. The sound stops as abruptly as it started and we hear thundering footsteps descending the stairs.

Alec, Ally, Kevin, Reese and Ty appear around the corner and run down the stairs.

I look at the others and then refocus on Richard.

"We don't have a choice anymore Finn, get her to the basement." His voice becomes a hiss. Finally I drop my eyes to the ground. A voice in my head whispers, telling me to listen to him. I already know what Scarlet would tell me to do, and that would be to listen to Richard. She stopped fighting for her own life a long time ago, and in her mind, this is her only out.

"Ah, so you're Finn." Kevin mutters eyeing me up and down. "Like a Shark fin?" he chuckles.

"Not now Kevin." I snap, I watch him jump a little and hide himself behind Alec.

"What's going on?" Alec asks.

"We're about to destroy the bunker." Richard explains briefly.

"With the bomb?" he asks Richard, searching his eyes. My

throat begins to grow tight.

Richard nods, "We've run out of other options."

"But...how would Scarlet get out? She'll die." Ally steps forward.

"He doesn't care." I mumble.

"What happened to the men that brought you here?" Richard asks, changing the subject.

"Out cold." Alec replies, shrugging like he knocks people out daily. Richard nods at him approvingly.

"We need to go." Kevin tugs Alec's arm urgently. He glances to the stairs and back. "They could wake up any moment."

"We've got at least thirty minutes." Alec responds. "And I'm not sure how I feel about this Scarlet issue."

"We don't have a choice." Richard tells him, trying to persuade him to take his side. Alec looks at me, awaiting my opinion. I just shake my head in defeat. I know that I can't convince Richard otherwise, even with Scarlet's life on the line. I also know that I can't change Scarlet's mind. Not once we tell her the plan.

"Where do we go?" Alec finally asks after realizing that I'm not going to reply.

"There's an emergency exit on six doors down from Scarlet's room, it's disguised at a dorm, few people know it's there. There are already rebels helping to evacuate the civilians, but if you're willing, they could use an extra pair of hands."

"You heard him." Alec barks out. "Let's get these people out of here."

All of them but Alec head off to find any people that still need evacuated. He stands, looking at me like he wants to tell me something, but he's interrupted by the sound of someone coming down the hallway. Richard raises a finger to his lips and guides us into a closet across the hall. We leave the door cracked open and watch as a solider drags Scarlet up the stairs. Alec's hand wraps around my wrist as if he could sense how much I wanted to kill that guard.

Once they'd disappeared from sight, Richard shimmies out of the closet and heads for the staircase. I attempt to follow, but Alec's hand remains on my arm, holding me back.

"Alec, I don't have time for this." I pull myself out of his grasp and turn to look at him. "Let me go save her." I beg. My eyes follow Richard as he climbs the stairs.

"I'm not going to stop you." he replies. "She might though."

"I know she will, but I have to try. It's a suicide mission. There's no way out."

"She knows that. She's known that this whole time Shark"

"I don't understand, how did we get here Alec? Why didn't we see this coming?"

"Anger drives people crazy and that girl is all anger." He stops talking.

"It didn't have to come to this though."

"No, it didn't. It should never have come to this." Alec sighs, "Look man, I don't know if this is the last time we'll see each other or if we'll by some miracle make it out of this." He takes a deeps breath and for a split second I believe I may have seen a hint of sorrow flash behind his eyes. "But incase we don't make it out in time, I just want to apologize for the things I said about Scarlet. You were right, she is family and I shouldn't have turned my back on you or her."

I offer him a pathetic smile in place of mushy words.

"But, don't make this the last time I see you." He forces a smile as he backs away from me. "Or Scarlet if you can help it."

"Thank you for everything Alec." I reply, as if I believe this is the last time we'll see each other. We salute each other and run off in opposite directions.

20

Scarlet

The man opens the door to a large room with an empty cell. Two men lay unconscious in front of the door. My escort shoves me into the cell and locks the door. I watch him pull out a hand gun I was unaware he was carrying. He scans the room carefully.

"Doctor, come in." he speaks into a watch on his left wrist.

I can't hear the doctor reply.

"They're gone. All of them, we have two men knocked out in here, I don't think." He checks them both for a pulse. "No, sir, they're still alive."

A pause.

"Yes, sir, the girl is in the cell."

Another pause as he listens to Doctor Fowler.

"Will do, sir." He turns to look at me and then scans the room one more time, his firearm still drawn. I begin to laugh slightly. I didn't mean to. But knowing that somehow they got out, somehow they're safe makes me so happy.

I don't care what happens to me now. I just want them to get out alive.

"What's so funny?" The man shouts at me, pointing the gun

in my direction. Something in me dares him to. Something tells me he's not supposed to be the one that kills me.

"Nothing." I reply calmly, stepping away from the bars.

He grunts, returning his focus to watching the room. Not long after his conversation with Doctor Fowler, Richard comes into the room. My heart sinks a little. I really want to like him.

"Jay, Nathan wants you to watch the entrance." he tells the man standing guard. Jay nods and marches out of the room.

"It seems as though you've gotten yourself on my brother-in-law's bad side." Richard says to me as he walks towards the cell door.

"It appears that way." I mumble, watching his every movement.

"That's something you and I have in common with one another." He unlocks the door. I continue to watch him. Is this a trick? "Nathan is power hungry and paranoid. He and I have not seen eye to eye for a long while. I do not believe that the mass murder of American citizens is how we should fix our problem."

"Then why do you work so closely with him?" I wonder. If they don't get along, why do I always see them together?

"For my family. But Scarlet, I'm afraid he's gone mad. After Carrie's death, he's been acting more irrational, more impulsive. However, I've heard you may have a way to stop him, or at least slow him down."

"I'm not sure what you want me to do."

"Scarlet, the research in this bunker is only in this bunker. The government doesn't even know about it yet. If we destroy it, we will slow down their efforts."

"You want me to use the bomb." I step out of the cell. He nods. "That will kill everyone inside."

"Yes, unless we get them out." he replies, "The walls of this bunker will contain the blast, and whatever chemical Evan put inside of the device."

"Richard, Nathan will catch us. We couldn't pull it off."

He begins walking towards the door. Hesitantly, I follow.

"Your friends have already started leading some out the emergency exit, Nathan assumes you only know of the front exit. All of his guards will be patrolling over there, I'm assuming he's been informed of your friends escape. You don't need to worry about the people, I just need you to get the bomb and detonate it." He opens the door, letting Finn in. "Finn is going to get you back to the lab. Once there, well, I hope Evan instructed you on what to do."

This is insane. How are we supposed to pull this off? I lock eyes with Finn.

"How much time do we have?" I ask Richard, still looking at Finn. Richard looks between the two of us and takes a deep breath.

"I suppose you two have five minutes to spare." He opens the door again and begins to leave. "Don't waste too much time. We have to be fast."

Five minutes. That's all we have. All I have to apologize, all he has to explain.

"Scarlet I..." he begins, stepping towards me.

"No, I know." I walk over to him and wrap my arms around him. "I forgive you. I know you weren't trying to hurt me." I cry a little as I feel him hug me.

"You don't have to do this you know." he whispers, knowing that if I detonate the bomb, I won't make it out. "Let me do it for you, please." I feel him trembling, listen to his breaths come out shaky.

"No." I shake my head. "I have to finish this Shark. This is my mission. I have to." He cries as he holds me. The two of us know this is the last time we will hold each other. I'm ready though, I'm ready to finish this.

I pull away from him and stare into his black eyes, my hands resting in his.

"This is for my parents and my friends and everyone they killed. This is for Kat." I tell him, tears rolling down my cheeks. "This is for everything we've lost. I have to do it." I breathe in. I look at the clock, we're almost out of time.

"Please Scarlet." he begs. "We can run and we'll be safe. You don't have to do it."

"And let more people suffer what we have? Shark, this could save lives."

"This will just slow them down Scarlet." He reminds me. "They'll do more research, they'll find a way."

"So you'll just have to find a way to stop them." I tell him. I offer him a smile. "Let me do this, so that you can find a way to save all those people." I squeeze his hands. "I wouldn't know how, but you, you're smart and you know how these people work. You could stop them from ever completing phase two. Shark, it can't be me, you have to be the one who gets out of here."

"No." he says breathlessly. "We can do this another way." He looks away from me for a moment, blinking tears out of his eyes. I look at the clock again and take a deep breath.

"We have to go." I tell him. "It has to be this way. You can't stop me."

He nods, I know he understands. He knows he couldn't stop me.

"I love you." I tell him.

"I love you too."

He kisses me for the last time. I close my eyes, imagining a different ending, an ending where I don't have to say goodbye to him. Where I don't have to break his heart like this.

"Alright. Let's do this." I squeeze his hand.

We continue to hold hands as we leave the room.

I'm scared but the adrenaline doesn't take long to kick in. After everything, I never really expected this to be how it ends. But I can't let more people die, not like this.

We jog down the hall, knowing we have to be fast.

As we pass another small hallway, I feel someone grab my arm. I pause and turn to see who's grabbing me.

"Scarlet." Alec says quietly. His expression is grave. He knows what we're doing.

"Alec, what are you doing?" I whisper. "You need to get out of here."

"For once, let me help you." he whispers back. "There are guards around the next corner. They're expecting one of us to come for the bomb." He warns us. Shark and I exchange a look. "It's only three of them, they're armed. But so am I." He shrugs, pulling out a handgun. I think for a moment. I want him to be safe, but I'm guessing I won't be able to get him to leave.

"Fine." I nod.

We continue walking, slower than before. Alec peeks around the corner, firing one shot into each guard faster than they could even pull theirs out. I stare at him in amazement. He smiles at me, shrugging it off.

"The lab's the last door in this hallway." Shark tells us, his voice faded. Alec and him exchange a look.

"Are you sure about this? We can still run."

"Shark." Alec places his hand on Shark's shoulder, "You can't stop her."

I'm surprised by Alec, I thought he would be on Shark's side.

"I know. I just...does it have to be done this way?"

We walk slowly towards the end of the hall. Every step harder than the last.

"We don't have time for anything else." I tell him. "It's now or never."

"But-" He begins.

"Shark." Alec cuts him off. We come to the door. I stare at it for a long moment.

The adrenaline has worn off, I'm terrified. My breaths become shaky again. My hand trembles as I reach for the handle.

"This is it guys, you should get out. I can do the rest." I turn to look at them. "It's okay."

Suddenly I hear a click. "Okay, maybe I should have seen you as a threat." Doctor Fowler comes up behind me, holding a gun to my head. I swallow hard, watching as Alec trains his gun on Fowler. "I'll have to admit. I didn't see that coming, you are quite the escape artist Scarlet. Finn, I'll have to say I'm rather disappointed in you. You grew up training to be a soldier, you were a loyal friend of mine. Are you really going to betray me? For a girl?"

"I don't want to have anything to do with this anymore." Shark growls, stepping forward.

"Let her go." Alec orders, his finger resting over the trigger. I just hope he can make the shot.

"Well Scarlet, aren't you popular?" Fowler scoffs. "No, I don't think I will let her go." I feel him press the end of the gun into my head. Alec looks at me, concerned. Can he make the shot? He has to, this can't be how this ends. If he shoots now, best scenario he shoots me instead. If he moves, Fowler will shoot. I have to move. I have to get out of the way fast, so Alec can make the shot. Shark moves to the side, reading my mind. Alec watches me, waiting to see what I'll do next.

"Shoot." I mouth to him.   He shakes his head slightly. "Shoot." I say audibly this time as I duck, hoping Alec can fire faster than the doctor can. *Bang*.

"Nice shot." Shark praises. I look behind me to see the Doctor's head resting in a pool of blood. An image of Kat appears as I close my eyes. *"I told you I wouldn't let you down."* I think to her ghost.

I open my eyes to see the two boys standing in front of me.

"So this is it." Alec says, dropping his gun to the ground. He embraces me in a hug. I don't react immediately, allowing my arms to stay by my sides until finally, I relax enough to hug him back. "I'm going to miss you Scarlet." he whispers. "But I understand."

"I don't understand." Shark interrupts us. "Why does it have to be like this?"

"Shark." I let go of Alec and turn to Shark. I rest my hand on his cheek.

"He's dead. Why don't we just set the research on fire and leave. We don't have to blow up the whole bunker." He gestures to Doctor Fowler's body. I consider his suggestion.

He's right. But if I'm honest, I'm tired. I'm ready for this, ready to be done. Is it the right answer? I honestly don't know...

it may not change anything. But I have to try.

"Shark, you know better than anyone that Doctor Fowler most likely has research and secrets all over this bunker. This is the only way to be sure that somebody else doesn't get their hands on this stuff. This is how I make sure *you* can save all those people." I caress his cheek. I'm sad to say goodbye to him, but I know if anyone can pull this off, it would be him.

"So set a timer and run."

"Evan never finished that part. Even if he had, who's to say the guards won't find it?" I look into his eyes one more time. "This is the only way we can be sure."

"I know…" he admits.

"Goodbye Shark." I smile. "It's been nice falling in love with you." I laugh lightly, my eyes beginning to tear up again. "Thank you for being my protection all this time."

"Thank you for being my hope." he replies, smiling back at me. His eyes are sad, but he understands. Maybe he understands more than he shows.

"Get him out of here." I calmly order Alec. He doesn't move right away, hesitant to let me do this.

"You got it boss." He smiles sadly. "Goodbye Scarlet." With that, he pats Shark on the shoulder and guides him in the other direction, leaving me to brave the rest of this alone.

"Give us like 15 minutes, so you don't blow us up. Okay?" Alec turns to call to me. I nod.

I watch the two of them disappear around the corner. My tears falling to the floor. I take one last look at Doctor Fowler as he lies, dead on the floor.

"I win." I smile at his corpse. Feeling victorious. Although, I'm not sure what kind of victory ends like this. I take a deep breath before opening the door. I walk slowly down the stairs to the lab.

The bomb rests on a desk in the middle of the room. I walk slowly towards it, checking the clock. I have fifteen minutes to sit here and think, fifteen minutes to change my mind. I pick the bomb up and sit cross-legged on the floor with it in my lap. I watch the clock, each minute feels like a day.

"I made it." I mutter to myself, leaning up against the desk. My mind wanders back to Alec's for the last time.

I reminisce about my first day there. Who knew it would all lead to this. I laugh as I remember Shark and I's date, the way he was so excited, the picnic. Our fight afterwards. I remember the night we were out in the desert telling stories and laughing together. I remember the time Ally met Sam. When we were all teasing her about her crush.

I don't want to think about the sad things anymore. I don't want to remember the time Evan attacked me or the morning I woke up to Alec telling me he was dead. I don't want to remember Alec's alcoholism or Kat's suicide.

The last few months that's been all I've remembered. Now, I want to remember the laughs, the smiles, the stories. This is for them, this is their happiness being avenged. This is us, saving other people's happiness, so the same story doesn't unfold for them.

I look at the clock, five more minutes. Deep breath. I can hear my heart beating in my ears. This is the last time I'll ever hear that sound, the last few breaths I'll ever take.

"Please Shark." I squeeze my eyes shut. "Please pull this off for me." I plead into the empty room. "I know this is gonna hurt, I know it does hurt, but please." I open my eyes.

Two minutes. I begin to tinker with the bomb, hoping I

remember what Evan told me to do. It's as though I can hear his voice in my head, walking me through it.

At this time, I feel the full guilt for not believing him.

"This is for you too, Evan. Sorry I got you killed." I whisper. I hold my finger over the button, shaking more than ever before.

"It's okay." I tell myself.

Last deep breath, last heartbeat. My finger presses the button. I hear a **click** and then a **beep**. I close my eyes. **Boom.**

I am consumed by fire and everything goes dark.

21

Shark

I look at the clock, we have fifteen minutes to get out of here. Alec and I run together in the direction of the exit. I can't believe this. I should be running towards her, talking her out of this. I shouldn't be letting her die alone.

"Keep going." Alec says as if he was just reading my mind. "I know it's hard to understand, but there's no stopping her. Now we just have to get out of here alive so we can finish what she's started." I know he's right, but it doesn't make me feel any better.

I think through our last couple conversations as we run. I remember the day she learned my real name. Hearing her call me Finn hurt. Shark was who I'd become in such a short time. Shark was the man that loved her, the man who put her above his mission.

Finn is a mindless sheep, a follower. Finn is a coward.

Ten minutes to get out of here, ten minutes before this place goes up in flames. We're close to the exit. It won't be long before we're out and safe. But she won't be safe, she'll be consumed by flames, burnt alive. I can't picture her like that. It hurts far too much.

A memory of our date back at Alec's flashes through my mind. I hadn't felt comfortable enough to show my affection before that day, but she deserved it, she deserved it all.

I'm gonna miss her smile. That smile was so sad all the time, but it was hopeful all the same. She has a way of making me feel hopeful, no matter what the situation. That's why we followed her so blindly, because she made us hope.

Not so much after Kat, but even then, she was still motivated. Eight minutes.

"Here we are." Alec opens the door that hides the emergency exit. "You first." He holds the door open.

I hesitate.

"I need to know you won't go back." he tells me.

I sigh, knowing that I probably would the second Alec stepped out the door.

It's bright outside. Sunny, as if the sky didn't get the memo that today is a dark day.

I check my watch, gifted to me by Doctor Fowler after I returned.

Five minutes. We walk further from the bunker.

The citizens are huddled together, preparing themselves to hear the explosion.

"She's not coming out, is she?" Ally asks me, taking my hand to comfort me.

"No." I swallow hard. I don't want to watch this. I don't want this to happen.

Ally begins to sob, Kevin joins in. I can't bring myself to cry yet. I just stare at the bunker, checking my watch every few seconds.

Two minutes. It's almost like I can hear her telling me she's sorry, begging me to finish this for her.

"I will Scarlet." I whisper. "I promise."

Ally squeezes my hand tighter. I don't turn to look at the others, I know they're crying.

Kevin places his hand on my shoulder as I count down in my head.

Less than one minute. I squeeze my eyes shut, praying that something will go wrong.

"Please don't work." I mutter.

Thirty seconds. Deep breaths. Part of me feels like I can hear her heart beating. Thumping in my head.

"It's okay." I whisper to her. "It's okay, don't be scared."

Boom.

I fall to my knees and sob into my hands. I can't hear her heartbeat anymore.

"*No.*" I think. "*It's not real.*" I try to convince myself.

Sure, I knew it was coming. Since the day she first met Nathan, I knew this would be the outcome. Nothing could have stopped her.

That's Scarlet for you, she sets her mind on it and nothing will keep her from doing it.

The others cover me as I cry. I know they feel it too. This emptiness. Scarlet was something special. She impacted all of our lives so much. She taught us to hope. She kept us going when we wanted to give up. She showed us how to feel again, after we'd been left numb from the attacks. She taught me how to love.

"Shark." Alec speaks after about thirty minutes. "She did the right thing."

Why is he so sure of that? I can see that going a million different ways, none of which involved losing her.

I wipe my face, tears still fall, but I stand. I look around at the group, all of them with tear stained faces. I stare at the bunker for a moment, smoke floats over top of it, but if you didn't know it had been bombed you wouldn't be able to tell, the outside looks the same as before.

Evening comes as we continue to cry and stare towards the bunker.

"Finn." Richard comes up beside me. "I know this isn't the best time. But the government will be sending people out any minute, they probably already know the bunker has been destroyed. We should try to find somewhere safe for the night."

"I know. You're right." I reply, not looking at him. "Have you spoken with everyone?" I ask.

"Yes, I've filled them in."

"And?"

"They—We are willing to follow your lead. They understand what's at stake." he replies. "Listen, Finn, I know this is hard. Scarlet meant a lot to you. But what she did may very well have saved more lives than you could count."

"I know." I look at the ground. Thinking of what to do next. I've never been much of a leader. I've always followed without question.

I look to Alec, he nods in approval.

"We'll follow you too." he tells me. The others nod reassuringly. I look back at the bunker before returning my gaze to Richard.

"Give me ten minutes." I tell them. "And then we'll head into the suburbs, there's a town about 4 hours away from here.

Get everyone ready to move."

I walk towards the bunker and sit in front of the door. I can still feel the heat radiating off of it. "That was by far the dumbest thing you've ever done." I say to her. "I knew you were driven, but really? I need you here. I don't know how to lead. They're looking to me to lead them in a war against the government. A war you started! Scarlet...this isn't fair! We need *you* to lead us."

I pause, waiting for a reply I know won't come.

"What could I have done? Could I have stopped you?" I ask. I know the answer, though. I couldn't have, nobody could have. She was convinced that this was the only way. I don't know, maybe she was right. But it doesn't feel fair. "They're gonna miss you too you know. Things will never be the same.

Who will we draw our strength from now? You with your bold hope that if we just kept working things would work out. They won't find that in me. You were the only hope I had left Scarlet. What do I do now? I know life wasn't kind to you. I know it hurt. I know, okay, I get it. But you didn't have to go that far. Did you?" I ramble to the door.

I pick up a rock and throw it forcefully at the door. I watch as it bounces off and lands back on the ground where it came from.

"Dammit it Scarlet, I really did love you. I would have traded you places if you had let me. I wanted to, I should have. You could've handled this next part, it didn't have to be me who lived. I can't do this like you did. I'm not brave and I'm not strong. Not without you." I stand from the ground and then I see her.

Of course I know it's not her, but her image. Covered in ash, her face blackened, her hands bloody. She smiles her sad smile at me and I feel at peace.

"Okay." I mutter. "Okay, I'll do my best." I tell her. "We'll take these guys down. For you, I will lead them." And then she's gone, but not totally gone. No, I won't carry her ghost with me until I die.

But she'll be here, giving me the hope I need to do this for them.

I turn to the others, the whole group of survivors from the bunker. They stand before me, waiting to take orders.

"Follow me." I tell them, walking in the direction of the nearest suburb. Alec and Ally and Kevin beside me. Reese and Ty behind me.

I lead them away from the bunker. Away from Scarlet, towards a new adventure.

Made in the USA
Monee, IL
17 January 2021